Being from Brooklyn, becoming a man in Baltimore, working in Hollywood, and then being born again...I can taste, feel, and smell every transition of this novel. Lady B. Moore is where the "Coldest Winter Ever" meets the "Prodigal Son".
-Kel Spencer, Emcee/Songwriter
(3rd Power Music Group)

"If you dare to be more, let Lady B. Moore show you how. It's a story so real and inspiring... you've got to read it."
-Doreen Spicer-Dannelly, writer/producer
(The Proud Family, Jump In!)

To Irina!
Remember? always
Be More! You are
going to laugh when
you read
about
Irina!

LIFE BEGINS WITH
GOOOD BOOKS™.

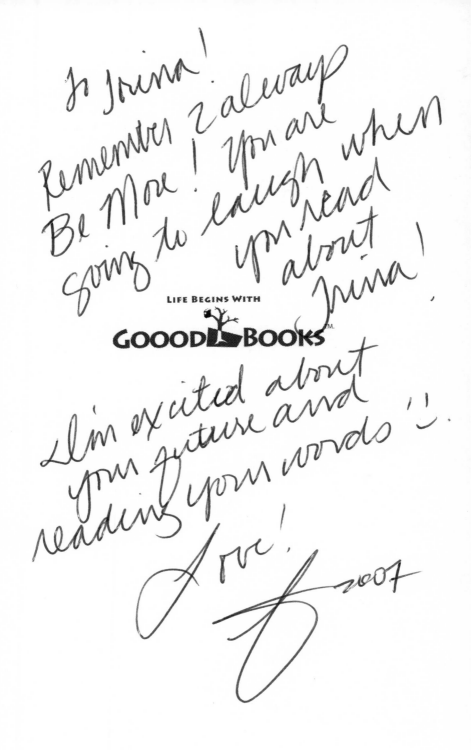

I'm excited about
your future and
reading your words "".

Love!

2007

Lady B. Moore

By TOVA

LIFE BEGINS WITH

GOOOD BOOKS™

PO BOX 91712
Los Angeles, CA 90009

This book is a work of fiction. Names, characters, places, and incidents are products of the author's imagination or are used fictitiously. Any resemblance to actual events or locales, or persons, living or dead, is entirely coincidental.

ISBN-13: 978-0-615-13410-9
ISBN-10: 0-615-13410-6

Cover design by Troy Cole and MeRhonda Ross

Edited by Sunny N. Fuller

Manufactured in the United States of America

For information regarding special discounts for bulk purchases, please contact Goood Books at gooodbooks@gmail.com

To those who want to "B" More...

Part One:
B.C.

Chapter 1:
Genesis

My momma named me Lady Belle Moore. Janice Moore was such a lady that she felt the need to impose her will upon me and make me her protégé by naming me something that I could never deny: "Lady Be More" (Lady B-More for all the local haters). Moms was "special"...not in a good way. Giving birth to me in between her addictions was the best thing she could ever have done. To this day, I still don't know how I didn't turn out to be a crack baby. She always told me that God "delivered" her from crack, because he had a special assignment for her life: to give birth to me.

Right after she had me, she started drinking and cheating on my father. *So*...God delivered her, then she gave birth to me to make my life a living hell while she floated in her habitual state of "high" by drinking and smoking weed everyday like coffee. Yeah...that really made a *whole* lot of sense. I would hope that God, who created heaven and earth, would've had enough sense to think of something better to do with His time than to create that hot mess.

I still don't understand why my father stayed

with my mother. According to him, it was love at first sight when he saw her. I am still trying to figure out what he saw—was it the crack pipe or the liquor bottle? I heard mom was the shit back then. I have to admit, she *was* a lil' hottie. She was about 5'6", chocolate brown with almond eyes, and had a big ol' butt with perfectly wide hips to match. She was really petite though. She always managed to keep a small waist. She had the longest, silkiest, pitch-black hair that flowed down to her bra strap. Her hair was always hooked. She kept her nails and feet perfectly manicured. She had the prettiest lips with a perfect pout. Her skin glowed and she didn't even have to wear make-up. Her high cheekbones defined her face. Everyone used to call her Cleopatra.

Now, I heard that my dad was really *fiiiiine*! He was light and sexy. My dad always worked out so he was always "cut." His hair always laid down smooth and he always kept a fresh shape-up. He had honey skin with freckles and sandy brown (almost red) hair. He was so fine that he was turning down ass. He always kept his clothes extra tight and he had the longest eyelashes. He would make all the women melt when he smiled and his dimples showed.

Ernest James Moore was the best dad ever! He was the sales director for a local radio station in Baltimore, Maryland. He worked so hard that he spent most of his time at work, but at least he paid the bills on time and made it to all of my important events. He met my mom, Janice, at a party in Odell's nightclub hosted by an old radio station he used to work for back in the day.

According to my dad, she was the finest thing he had ever seen. He told me that his first thought when he saw her was to blow her back out and have her scream his name. My dad was a realist and he talked to me "real." He told me that after he chased her down all night and finally talked to her, he was in love. He found out that she was the owner of the two major hair salons in the city, Another Level Salon and Another Level Salon Phase 2. He also said that he never met a woman who was so smart with a body that would make a nigga scream *her* name just by looking at her. And to really put the "cherry-on-top", she was a "church-girl". What he didn't see was that she was a functional drug addict.

After only six months of dating my mother, he proposed. He was already paying all of her bills along with half of both shop's expenses. Moms told him that she felt convicted about having sex with him before marriage. Dad said that the sex was so good that he *had* to put a ring on my mom's finger just so she wouldn't share it with anyone else.

My mom went to church every Sunday, served on the usher board, and partied *hard* every Friday night. Dad started going to church with my mom and he got saved. Everyone envied my parents' relationship. Dad was established doing sales at a local radio station and my mom was the flyest woman in B-more. They had money, always wore the latest designer clothes, drove matching Camaros, and looked "the bomb" together. That's what my daddy used to tell me. Every woman in B-more was hot with jealousy. Even though their men were ballin', they still had to live that hustler's life. Everyone knew that most men who were ballin' in B-more were doing their "thang-thang" (selling drugs). They were envious that she lived better than them and didn't have to worry about her man getting locked up or getting shot.

They got married a year after meeting at the party and my mom got pregnant with me a month after the wedding. I instantly became a "daddy's girl." Daddy couldn't wait until I turned three months old, so he could put some diamond earrings from Tiffany & Co. in my ears. As soon as I grew out of my walking shoes, my daddy got them plated in gold and had them dangling from the rearview mirror in his Camaro. He used to tell me that while all his friends wanted lil' boys, he wanted a lil' girl. He wanted to teach me how to reverse the game on these lil' niggas out here who called themselves players. He would take me out on "dates" when he could, and just tell me the real.

He didn't hold anything back from me, including why he chose moms to be his wife: she made him wait longer than any woman he ever tried to "hit" (have sex with). My mom said that my dad was a cold-piece, and that she finally gave in, because he was so persistent. Plus, he was doing a lot for her and they weren't even together yet. She refused to be his girlfriend.

My dad said that my mother was the most trust worthy, reliable, loving person he had ever met. I guess she failed to tell him one small but very important detail about herself–GOD "delivered" her from crack just two months before their wedding. She was supposed to stay drug free, but she had a relapse and got hooked again on my first birthday.

My dad found out she was a functional drug addict when she failed to pick me up one time from day care. She was always picking me up from day care, and then dropping me off at my grandma's house so she could go back to work at her shop. She would always say that she had a lot of clients, and then wouldn't pick me up until 2AM the next morning. Daddy suspected that she was having an affair, so he called one of his police buddies to get the address of an unfamiliar number on our house phone bill.

So when my mom "forgot" to pick me up from day care again, he went to the house of this unfamiliar phone number after he dropped me off at my grandma's house. He knocked on the door and when this young lil' nigga answered, daddy knocked him out on his own floor and walked into his house. He found my mother butt naked with a needle stuck in her arm, knocked out sleep. He got so furious that he pulled out a knife from the dude's kitchen and tried to kill him until the dude's eight year-old daughter walked in from school, screaming and crying from all the commotion. He dragged mom out of the house by her hair as she begged for her needle. From that moment on, my dad knew that she wasn't as perfect as she made her self seem.

When she sobered up and saw that my dad was packing up all of his stuff to leave, she begged him to stay and told him that the devil was trying to destroy what they had. She told him that she loved him and that she would never cheat or shoot up again. Well, she didn't lie. She just became a functional alcoholic. So hundreds of almost thousands of liquor bottles later, my dad Ernest has been married to my mom Janice for over twenty-something years. Ernest and Janice Moore—isn't that the perfect love story?

I still don't know how she managed to hide her addictions from the church and everyone else over the years. It was hard for me *not* to notice she had a problem when I spent most of my childhood walking over her on the kitchen floor to get to the refrigerator in the morning before school. She would fall off of the chair from drinking too much. I have to admit that she was the most functional alcoholic I'd ever seen. Even though she made a lot of money from running her two hair shops, she barely bought me anything...not even a chicken box. I went to my dad for everything: money, clothes, bras, panties, MAC lip glass...*everything*. It was pathetic.

The only time she would cook was during the holidays, and when she would make breakfast for herself at two in the morning. I would hear the sound of pots and pans making all this noise while I was trying to sleep. Then, she would come to my room and try to wake me up, asking me if I wanted some cream chipped beef. She used to get on my *last* nerve.

When she was sober, she raised me up to be this perfect lady and schooled me on how to play the game when it came to boys. She used to always say, "NEVER fall completely in love, NEVER give him your heart, NEVER tell him everything (especially how many sex partners you've had), NEVER check his voicemail (unless you really want to find something), NEVER give it up before three months (if you do, wait at least three months before the next time to make up for the slip up), and NEVER say "never". Oh and one important thing—the only real commitment is marriage. Boyfriends always cheat."

When I graduated from college, amazingly enough I was still a virgin. Being a 22-year old virgin in B-More was unheard of until I came along. You would think that my household situation would leave me no choice but to follow in the footsteps of my alcoholic mother and my disillusioned father. It was the exact opposite. I grew up during most of my youth as a nerd and a late-bloomer.

However, by the time I got to college I was the shit. I was about 5'6", had the complexion of honey, big light brown eyes with long eyelashes, and long, silky, mahogany brown hair. I was the captain of Morgan State University's cheerleading team, a dance team member, and I graduated with honors. I had that bangin' body, I was sexy as hell, and I was on my way to Los Angeles to become the best-damned choreographer the industry had ever seen.

My dad thought I had lost my mind by

thinking I was gonna move to L.A and be a music video dancer. But I wasn't going to do just *any* video; I was going to take dance and videos to another level. My mom always kept my hair tight (I always wore a long roller set wrap), and I could dance better than any bitch out there. Besides, I had the street smarts mixed with book smarts to do it. I was determined to leave for L.A. as soon as possible. I had talked about it the whole time I was in college and had saved up about $3,000. My flight left tomorrow.

"Lady," dad said as we sat in the living room, "You really need to think this out."

"I *have* thought it out, dad. I'm going." I was grown. What was he gonna do, really?

"Of all places to go to after college, you choose L.A.? There's nothing good out there for you. You want to dance in those videos where every single girl looks like a damn tramp, all half naked?"

"You've raised me well. I'm going to be selective with what videos I do dad - - "

"From what I've seen on AET and NTV, you don't have *that* many fuckin' choices, Lady! Either you're the girl fondling the rap stars or the half naked hooch laid out on some pimps' car! I better not see you shakin' yo' ass in one of those poolside videos, talkin' 'bout this is dance, THIS IS ART! This is *bull shit*!" My dad was turning bright red.

"I'm going dad," I said firmly, without any sign of emotion.

He was so furious that he knocked the living room chair over and slammed the back door as he left. My mom sat quietly in the living room and looked at me intently. I knew she was about to turn into her fifth personality, Sister Saint Janice (the bona fide church girl.)

"Lady, God won't ever leave you," my mom interjected.

"Mom, I really don't feel like hearing the church talk right now."

"As long as you know in your heart that you want to go, then go. Your dad will understand. I know Jesus will be with you wherever you go."

"Mom, dad has never slammed the door in my face. Can Jesus save me from Ernest don't f-wit-me' Moore?"

Her answer to everything was Jesus. I am still trying to figure out how an alcoholic can direct me to heaven. Does she really think she's goin'?

"You're his only child. You know you're daddy's little girl," my mom said.

"Yeah? Well, that's the point. I ain't little...I'm grown. I finished college for him. I ain't gonna live my life for him too, and I definitely ain't stayin' another minute in B-More."

"It's a lot of pressure, Lady. He's the deacon of the church now, and going to L.A. to become a dancer isn't exactly what your dad has in mind as earning a good Christian living."

"Whatever. Excuse me, I need to go pack."

I guess her being sober wasn't mandatory either. I was tired of my mother telling me what the good "Christian life" was supposed to be. I haven't been to church regularly since the age of twelve. I knew at an early age what a hypocrite looked like. I lived with one every day.

I believed in God, I just didn't believe that God would be in a place like church. The preacher's daughter was the biggest ho in B-more, the same gay guy would catch the holy ghost every Sunday, and almost everyone talked about the new person who just got saved and how much of a mess they were right after they came from the alter. Whenever someone gave a testimony, you could surely believe that their business would be in the streets within the hour. Certainly Jesus couldn't be in a place like that. He would have to be *outside* of the church door, trying to flag people down to go the other way, saying "Run for your lives if you want to be saved, DO NOT come in here!" And then I could see Satan, all dressed up in his pimp suit, on the sidewalk saying "Step right up! Come one, come all. It's the 'goin' to hell' circus! The only price you pay is your best monetary offering."

My dad said that it would have been wrong if he left my mother. He said that divorce was just not allowed according to the Bible, and that he was supposed to love my mother like Christ loved the church. Why would Christ or anybody with good sense love the church? I know Jesus ain't retarded. One thing was for sure; I wasn't going to end up being like the group of depressed adults I grew up around.

I went to my room to pack. I looked around really hard one last time. I realized that it was the last time I was going to sleep here. I had a true princess room. A flowing canopy bed with matching curtains that always made me feel safe at night. In the summer it would blow and look like angels dancing around in my sleep.

Mom believed that every woman should be extra lady-like. She always made sure my clothes, room, and I were the epitome of class. She definitely "looked" the part. She was a lady in public and a nightmare at home. Don't get me wrong...I loved my mother. I just thought that she was a tad bit selfish. How could she choose shootin' up and gettin' drunk over me? She would always say (especially when she was drunk), *"I love you more than anything in this world."* She used to say it so much that I thought she was trying to convince herself. I surely didn't believe it.

Chapter 2: Church Folk

Ring.

"Hello?" I answered, ear to my pink fluffy phone.

"I got you a gig, girl!" Trina yelled.

Trina Parker was my best friend. She had been living in LA for about a year, and she and I were going to be roommates.

"Stop lying!" I screamed. I couldn't believe it.

"I ain't lyin!" she said. "You start as soon as you get out here."

"What is it? Who I'm dancin' wit'?"

"The new rapper, and my baby, Lord Life."

"Trina, I know it's not for that song that just came out called 'Bang It'…"

"Yeah, and…?" she said firmly.

"I don't know, Trina. I mean, the track is hot, don't get me wrong…"

"Look, Lady. I went out of my way to get you in. I promised Lord you were super cute. I told him you could dance your ass off. God is already looking out for you. Plus, you got lead dancer in the dance segment if they like what they see. Plus, girl, he would do anything for me and I put myself on the line to get you in."

"Yeah, Trina. I'll see you tomorrow."

"I'll pick you up from LAX at 11 a.m."

"Aight, girl." I hung up.

Trina always went to church. I met her in church in B-more and her parents were really close to my parents. Trina was always like a big sister to me and would look out for me, no matter what. She sang on the choir most of her life and everyone loved her. She had decided to move to L.A. the year before to pursue acting and singing. She would always try to get me to go church. She knew almost all of the Bible stories. To top it off, she was the pastor's daughter. Yeah, she was the ho. She had a good heart though. She would act like a perfect angel in church but I knew the truth.

Pastor Parker used to preach about how men in the church had a duty to keep their families in order. He would preach about how lovely his family was, and every Friday night Trina and I would sneak down to the Paradox nightclub and dance hard until 3 a.m. She used to spend the night at my house because my mom would hang out and my dad would work late every Friday. He would spend the night at the office a lot because he used to be too sleepy to drive home. My dad worked so hard.

Those were the days. Clubbin' in Baltimore was better than any club experience in the country. First, we had our own club music. Frank Ski, (the city's hottest deejay ever), took R&B/Rap music, sped the track up really fast, then added in some more bass and beats and club music was born. My favorite song was "Out My Way, Bitch." Man, when that song used to come on, Trina and I would push our way through the club screaming, *"Out my way, bitch -- ahhhhhh! Out my way, bitch – ahhhhhhhh! Don't you see I'm tryna get through?"*

Since we had our own music, we also had our own dances. I think B-more was the only place where it was normal to rub, grind, and back your butt so hard on a guy's dick that it would make him hard. Trina and I used to dance real hard with guys, and as soon as we felt a nigga get hard, we would move to the next guy. I was going to miss Baltimore. I was going to miss chillin' at Lexington Market. I knew LA didn't have chicken boxes with salt, pepper, ketchup, and hot sauce. Dang, man…

As I started to pack, my dad appeared in the doorway. "Lady," he interrupted. "I know you don't like going to church, but you need to go to Bible study tonight with the family one last time."

"Ok," I said, without looking at him.

"Lady, I am proud of you. You finished college and even though I don't agree with what you are doing by moving to LA, I am proud of you."

"Yes, Dad."

"Be ready in an hour."

Man! I was not feelin' going to church with those hypocrites right before my break to L.A.
■■■

"Pastor Parker really broke it down this evening, didn't he?" Sister Williams said, talking to my mother. My parents always liked to stand around after the service to talk with the other church members. You would think they would've gotten tired of talking to the same dry people every week. Didn't they just see everybody on Sunday?

"And we haven't seen you in a while, Lady," Sister Williams directed to me. "I hear you're moving to L.A. tomorrow."

"Yes, Sister Williams," I said politely. Sister Williams was this big fat lady who stank. She was about my height and light skinned, with the fashion sense of a horse. She actually looked like a horse, come to think of it. She smelled like mothballs and fish. She was always offering her opinion to everyone like she knew it all. I knew one thing — she needed a super douche and a bath.

"Make sure you find yourself a good church home," she said to me. "The temptations in Hollywood are strong. You need a good church covering to keep you safe from the attacks of Satan."

I looked at her. *Was I supposed to comment to her statement?*

"I am telling you Lady," she continued. "Get in church. The end is near and there's a quick route to hell. Oh yes, Jesus...hmmmm...thank you, Holy Spirit. God is speaking to my heart to tell you right now, Lady. God has a plan for you. God is my witness, I am going to prophesy to you right now..."

I would've preferred that she didn't right then. I mean, did she ask if I wanted to hear what she had to say? It wasn't Hollywood that I was worried about. It was *her* crazy tail. She used to roll around the floor every Sunday, foaming at the mouth and screaming. To top it off, she used to grab her son, Tim, and run out of the church to the trash can in the hallway screaming, "Satan, come out of him! In the name of Jesus, come out!!" Yeah, I *really* wanted to hear this one...

"God said that the kingdom of heaven is near to those who obey his *every* word," she warned. "He's coming back for a true church. Lady, make sure you're in church so that when Jesus comes back you'll be lifted up with the other saints of God."

"Sister Williams, I need to be a member of a church in order for that to happen?"

"As God is my witness! Oh thank you, Jesus...yes, Lord! Lady, get you a church home. You need to join a church. I'm gonna pray for you."

"Thank you, Sister Williams," I said calmly. Was she serious? God was coming back to take everyone up in church to heaven? Now, I definitely knew I was not joining anybody's church. I also knew that I was not trying to spend eternity with those simple folks. Was she for real?

"Lady, thank you for coming," my dad said as soon as Sister Williams left.

"You're welcome, Dad."

"We're going to leave as soon as I find your mother. I know she's around here somewhere, letting someone talk to her until I come over and interrupt the conversation. Oh, there she is…"

My mom was talking to First Lady Parker at the front of the church. I knew they were probably talking about Trina and I living together.

"Come on, Lady. Let's grab your mother and go," my dad said with urgency.

We walked over to them and my dad smoothly said, "Well, I hate to interrupt the two finest ladies in town, but my two ladies need their beauty sleep. They certainly have to keep up with your good looks, First Lady Parker."

"Oh stop it, Ernest. Janice, you'd better get this old charming husband of yours." First Lady Parker had the biggest grin.

First Lady Parker was smiling a little too hard in my opinion. She smiled so hard that I could see her wisdom teeth. A wise woman knows not to seem that anxious about a compliment. That was *way* too needy. I was ready to go.

"Miss Lady B. Moore, Trina is going to be a good role model for you," she said, switching the subject.

It was a shame that First Lady Parker didn't know that her precious daughter, and my best friend, switched men as often as First Lady Parker got her hair done every week.

"Yes, I am really excited about it, Mrs. Parker."

"You two are going to do so well. I just want Trina to get more involved with those touring Christian plays. She needs to be using that gift that God gave her for the kingdom. I just hope she continues to be selective with her choices of roles out in Hollywood."

Had First Lady Parker seen the latest music video that Trina was in? I doubted they had seen it, because they kept their channel cemented on TBN. Trina was tastefully half naked as the lead girl in the Big Red video. She wasn't gyrating or anything, but I knew the Parkers wouldn't have approved of her wearing a skirt as long as underwear for three minutes straight on national TV.

"I am confident that she will do just that, Mrs. Parker," I responded.

"Excuse me, but we really need to go," my dad firmly interrupted.

"I'll call you, Pam," my mom politely said.

"Alright, Sister Janice." First Lady Parker winked at my mom.

I was so happy to see my daddy put his foot down so I could leave that foolish place. This was why I had been M.I.A. (missing in action) from the church since I was twelve. I used to be on the choir and everything. I would go to church only if my dad begged me to go. Dad used to always say that Jesus was in the heart and not in a building. Well, he certainly couldn't have been in *that* building, and I found it hard to believe that he would last half a second in the hearts of "**church folk**."

On our way home in the car, I reflected on how I grew up in B-more. I laughed when I remembered how we used to crack on the way the

Chinese folks who owned the sub shop in Edmondson Village would say, "You want sul, peppa, kesshup?" when we would order a chicken box. And I loved going to my grandma's house in the Village. Dang, I *knew* they wouldn't have egg custard flavored snowballs in L.A. And don't let me get started on the nine o'clock mix on 92Q — that was my joint! Trina and I used to dance our butts off in my room back in the day. Oh, and especially when New Year's Eve would come around, the radio would be rockin'! Dang. So, was I gonna have to listen to all that west coast rap all day? The only rapper I would dare rock from the west coast was Tupac, and he was originally from B-more. He even graduated from the high school that I graduated from: The Baltimore School for the Arts.

I knew I was destined for greatness. People from B-more who made it in the industry shut it *down*. I was gonna be next.

Chapter 3:
Sweet Thang

"Ladies, let's go inside," daddy said, as he pulled up the emergency brake of his black Infiniti Q45. We lived in Ashburton in West Baltimore. It was actually a nice neighborhood. However, no matter where you lived in B-more, you could never escape the ghetto. I would walk down the street like ten minutes and see niggas standin' out on the corner, especially in the summer. Shoot, Trina and I used to take walks for twenty minutes just to see the "sights." We had a really large single home. The lawn was manicured really well. We had a traditional brick house with white shudders. Mom loved to plant these dainty lookin' flowers that would be so pretty in the spring. We had a nice sized porch with wicker furniture. Dad chained the furniture to the pole connected to the porch in case some wandering crack heads decided to get happy and use the furniture to get high. (I knew Dad had paid a grip for our porch set.) I loved our house, I loved our neighborhood, and I loved B-more.

As I was getting out of the car, I noticed that someone was sitting in a truck pulled behind us. I looked really hard and saw that it was John

Anderson sitting in the front seat, smiling. I couldn't believe my eyes, when I saw how *fine* he looked. As he got out of his Ford Expedition, I almost passed out. He was about 6'2" and brown-skinned. His haircut was fresh. He had on a green La Coste polo shirt, a pair of dark blue jeans, and some white and green La Coste sneakers. Then he had the nerve to wear this bangin' Gucci silver watch that perfectly complimented his outfit. He walked over to me with this manly swagger, smiling with those sexy dimples, (just like my daddy).

I was glad I never left the house without being "on point", especially at a time like that. My hair fell perfectly with my fresh roller set wrap. I had on my silver Tiffany bracelet, silver studded Tiffany earrings, silver Tiffany necklace, coconut colored pencil skirt, chocolate colored peek-a-boo toe wedge heels, and a candy apple red shirt that perfectly accented my honey complexion. Then, I had a nerve to rock this bangin' chocolate colored clutch purse to set it off. I was a tough force to be reckoned wit'.

"Lady," John looked me in the eyes. His eyes were dancing—oh yeah, that nigga was ON me.

"John," I smiled. He knew I was the shit.

"Lady Belle...still holding true to your name, I see." He smiled as I gazed at his broad shoulders and stocky build. It was confirmed; he was nibbling at the bait.

"Well, if it isn't my man John Anderson!" my dad interrupted as he practically ran over to shake his hand.

"Hello, sir," John said firmly.

"Now, you know you can call me Mr. Ernest. You practically family, boy! I heard you graduated from Hampton last year!"

"Yes, sir. Mrs. Williams from church told me that Lady was moving to L.A. tomorrow, so I had to make my way over here." John said, as he smiled at me.

See how fast word would travel with folks in Baltimore, and especially in the church? You might as well have just plastered my face with a big ol' grin on the front of the Baltimore Sun Newspaper. I could see the headline: "Lady Belle Moore, the 22-year-old virgin, goes to Hollywood."

"And I see Mrs. Moore is still running the city," John said. He smiled at my dad. I knew the only thing moms was running was the streets.

"Well, look who just turned out to be Mr. Charming." Mom smiled as she patted John on his back. John would always just stare at my mom. I think that if she had been a little bit younger, I would have had some genuine competition.

"So, I heard you just opened your own barbershop," dad added.

"Yes, sir. I'm also promoting different events around Baltimore."

"Now that's what I'm talking 'bout, player. I'm gonna have to come check you out and get a shape up." Dad shook John's hand. "Well, I'm gonna finish some paperwork at the office. I will see you all later tonight." He turned to my mom. "I'll be home around twelve. I promise I won't work too hard, sweetie." He kissed my mom goodbye.

"Night, babe," mom smiled at dad as he walked off. Then she turned to us. "Goodnight, you two. Don't forget to finish the load of laundry you got sitting in the basement, Lady."

"Yeah, aight, Mom." Did she really have to put me on blast like that? I mean dang...I wasn't little. I *knew* I had to finish packing. She really got on my nerves.

"So...word on the streets is that you're doin' your thang-thang." I smiled at John.

"Oh, so you the FBI now?" John said seriously.

"Naw. Trina just told me that you were hustlin' while you were at Hampton, and then you moved back after school to open up your own business to cover your tracks."

"What's Trina's nosy ass doin' all in my business all the way from Cali? You'd better watch her. She need to keep her mouth off of my dick. She got wack ass head game, anyway."

"Oh *really*..." I said. Dang, Trina let John hit too? No wonder I was still a virgin. She was always running through every nigga I even thought about kickin' it wit'.

"Yo, Trina hit my boy off. I would never let that run down horse even suck my shit."

"John!" I punched him in his chest.

"Yo, you know Trina's a ho. That ain't no secret. How you think she got in that Big Red video? She looks like a horse with make-up. She do got a phat ass, though."

"John!!!" I punched him again. "Yo, kill it. Ain't nothing changed, you still ignorant as hell."

John laughed so loud that I had to punch him again. His big mouth was gonna wake up every nosy neighbor on my block.

"Speaking of no change, I hear you *still* savin' it."

"Bye, John…" I started to leave.

"Lady—c'mon, lil' momma. I didn't mean it like that. I mean, that's good."

John pulled me close in his arms and hugged me. Okay, I did not remember John being cut up like that before. DAMN! I had no choice but to melt in his arms. I think my eyes sort of rolled to the back of my head a lil' bit. John Anderson sure wasn't "little" anymore.

"What's all this for?" I smiled in a flirting way.

"We grown, and I see you ain't little no more."

"Likewise," I responded. I thought to myself, *Is this nigga reading my mind?*

"If you're not too busy, we can go grab something to eat before you head in."

"I guess…" I said with a smirk.

"I guess!? *Shit*, I can save my money," John smiled. "But I'd rather spend it on the woman I'm tryna get at."

"C'mon, player.... Nigga, don't think cause you got some chips now and you lookin aight, I'm supposed to be jockin' you. I remember when your lil ding-a-ling fell out your shorts when you were playin' ball at Druid Hill Park in high school."

"My shit ain't little. You comin' or what?"

"Is *that* the way to talk to a lady?" I smiled.

"Excuse me, bring yo' ass. You know you feelin' me."

"Whatever. Hold on." I pulled out my silver cellie and called my mom.

Ring.

"Yes, Lady," my mom answered.

"Ma, I'm bout to go eat wit' John. I'll be back."

"Remember you still have to pack—"

"Aight, ma..." I cut her off.

Click.

I hung up and turned to John.

"Let's go..."

John opened my door, I jumped in and we were off.

He was blastin' Jay Z's album Reasonable Doubt. That album was a classic. Trina and I would have that album on repeat when we used to visit our girl in Brooklyn every summer. Four hours of heat in the speakers...WHAT?!

We pulled to a red light and a group of guys on my side was staring all into the truck. I *did* look good in John's truck. John saw the guys staring, so he turned down his music, rolled my window all the way down and looked right at them without blinking.

"Is there a fuckin' problem? Somethin' wrong wit' yo eyes partner?" John said casually. I had never heard a man talk so forcefully without even raising his voice—no man besides my pops, of course. Shit, I was scared. The guys in the car next to me just looked away and didn't say anything like some straight punks.

"Yeah, I thought so," John said loud enough for them to hear. He rolled up my window and turned the radio back up. He grabbed my hand.

"You aight?" he looked at me.

"Yeah," I smiled.

I'd known John since I was like eleven. We went to the same middle school. His folks used to live right across the street from us until they got divorced when he was in high school. His mom moved to Randallstown and his pops eventually got locked up for hustlin' when John was like sixteen. John learned everything he knew about the streets from his dad before he split and got locked up a year later. To this day, everyone wonders if John's mom set his pops up, because he was trying to leave her to be with a younger woman. John's dad was such a good "business-man" that somebody had to have snitched.

John used to come over to my house faithfully. Trina, John, Mook, (short for Michael), Keisha, Tee Tee, Rob and I used to roll tight back in the day. Trina, Keisha, Rob and I used to go to the Baltimore School for the Arts. Tee Tee went to

Western High School and was in The Fashionettes like all four years. We used to show off at the fashion shows. Western fashion shows were the biggest fashion shows in the city.

Keisha was the craziest chick I ever knew. We used to sneak in the club, and she used to keep a razor under her tongue in case she needed to slice some ho's face who was tryin' to talk shit. She didn't play. She wasn't gonna use the razor to kill. She was just gonna make sure that whoever fucked wit' her was gonna remember it for the rest of their lives with some permanent marks on their faces. Keisha's mom was a straight up crack head. We used to go visit Keisha down on Division Street, and her mom would come outside and yell, "Aaaay Keisha!!!!!!! Ca' mere, *biiitch*!" We never stopped laughing about that. Shit, if you could survive growin' up in B-more, you could survive anything. By the time I was in the tenth grade, I had already had somebody pull a gun out on me. After feeling cold steel on my side, I was numb to what would scare the shit out of most people.

John and Mook were best friends. John went to Poly and Mook went to Walbrook. John and Mook were always real smart, but they also had mad street smarts. Even back then, nobody would fuck wit' those two, especially Mook. Mook was one crazy ass nigga.

I remember when like ten niggas downtown at the Harbor rolled up on Mook and John and tried to bank them (fight them). They pushed us girls out of the way and started swinging back. John was stomping this one nigga in the head while the nigga's two friends were trying to swing on John to get him off of him. Mook laid out like two niggas and then picked up a broken brick from the steps and beat the shit out of this one dude until you could see the dude's white meat. The side of his head was all bloody. The dude's friend called himself banging Mook in the arm. You could tell his friend was scared as hell. Mook finally decided to pull his gun out after he had beat down like three niggas, and John had beat down like two. The rest of the guys who tried to beat up John and Mook ran off when they saw the gun. Mook picked up the brick he used to beat the nigga with and took it with him, talking bout, "Niggas need to know…fuck this…I need a souvenir for this shit." We ran all the way to Saratoga Street to get on the 23 Bus Stop. That was the story of the year.

After high school, we all went to college except for Mook. Tee Tee got pregnant her twelfth grade year, but still went to Howard while her mom took care of her daughter during the school year. Tee got married right after college and we didn't talk to her as much. Everyone pretty much didn't talk everyday like we used to when we went to college. Trina and I talked everyday because we were best friends. We still talked everyday, even after she moved to L.A. I stayed on campus, so Trina would always fill me in on everything.

Mook got into the streets hard and started getting real greedy. John was just selling weed on the low on campus at Hampton while Mook started getting into major shit. John would come home a lil' once and a while to help Mook out. They always rolled hard no matter what. When John was away at campus, a group of new guys on the block acted like they were trying to get into the game with Mook and set him up. Mook was shot and killed on his 20th Birthday. John never really got over that too much, and he never trusted anyone after that.

Trina told me that he hustled real hard when he got out of college, and eventually started to leave all the major shit alone once he made enough money. Then, he opened up his own businesses so that he could eventually give the game up. A year after he graduated college, he opened up his own barbershop on Liberty Road. John had also started promoting the hottest "white linen" parties of the summer. He was doin' it big to be so young.

My dad knew that John was doing his "thang-thang", and he used to give him advice. I would hear them in the basement. My dad kinda stepped in when John's dad got locked up. That's why he used to love coming over to my house.

"You want to go to Little Italy? We can go to Da Mimmo," John asked.

"That's cool," I said.

Now this nigga was showing off. That was one expensive ass restaurant.

Chapter 4:
Truth

We drove past the Inner Harbor. We used to go down there almost every holiday when it was crowded and just crack on folks. We pulled up to valet and hopped out of the truck. John held my hand the whole time until we sat down at our table.

We sat at a nice, cozy little table in the corner. It was kinda funny to peep John's game. It was hard for me not to look at him as lil' John John; however, his newfound confidence and sense of awareness about everything helped me to see him as a man. He paid very close attention to every detail about every single thing.

There was some live music playing and a woman walking around selling roses. It was pretty *live* for a Wednesday night. We sat in a cozy corner and I was lovin' it.

I looked across the room and saw a man who looked like my dad, sitting there with a light-skinned, really pretty and nicely dressed woman.

"John, doesn't that look like my dad?" I said, trying to check things out.

"Uh, yeah, that's him. She's probably one of his clients from the radio station."

Yeah, it was like nine o'clock at night, but I knew salesmen did whatever they needed to do to get the business. My dad *got* the business.

"What the fuck!?" I said, in disbelief.

I was looking over to where my dad was, and he was stroking the woman's cheek while kissing her. It was nowhere near a peck, either. Then she rubbed the top of my dad's head while he pulled her closer. I couldn't believe that shit! All that talking he did about him loving mom like Christ loved the church. So, was he telling me that Jesus was a pimp? What the fuck!?

"Yo, Lady — you aight?" John asked.

"Let's go." I didn't even wait for John to come along. I just grabbed my purse and I practically ran out of the restaurant. I was so hurt. Maybe, it was a mistake. Maybe, it wasn't him. There had to be something that my folks weren't telling me. Maybe, they were planning on getting a divorce because my mother's addictions were too much and they hadn't told me yet. I could feel the tears welling up in my eyes. As soon as we got in the truck, I broke down and started crying. John pulled over.

"Come here," John told me, as he pulled his seat back. I crawled over to his lap. I just sat in his arms and wept. I was so embarrassed. I was in denial. Not *my* dad. All those talks he had given me about faithfulness and sticking by your mate no matter what. John grabbed my chin and began to kiss me.

"I want to go home," I interrupted.

We got to my house in less than fifteen minutes. I just wanted to go to my room and pack. My house was already dysfunctional, and now this just put it over the top. John walked me up to my door to make sure I got in okay.

"Call me if you need me," John said. "I'll have my phone on in case you need to call."

"Thanks, I should be okay," I replied. I waved goodbye and ran to my room. I blasted my music and started packing. It took me about two hours to finish up everything except for the clothes that were in the dryer downstairs. By that time it was around 12:30 am and mom was asleep. It was clear for me to go downstairs, without Sister Saint Janice scoping me out. She always could tell when something was wrong. I turned off the light in my room and walked downstairs in the darkness in case someone was up. I didn't feel like being bothered. As I was coming up the stairs from the basement, I could hear my mom and dad whispering in the living room.

"Look, Ernest, I'm sick of yo' shit!" Mom was stumbling over her words, drunk. "It's thirty minutes past fucking midnight. I'm not young and dumb anymore, muvafucka!"

"Janice," he hushed her. "Look, baby. You cannot keep making me pay for something I did over twenty years ago! Look, baby—I was at a meeting and I had to run to the office to finish up some paperwork."

That son of a bitch. I lifted up so that I could see the lies in action. Mom was shaking and dad was moving in close to her and rubbing her cheek that same way he was rubbing that skank ho's cheek at the restaurant an hour before.

"You cheated on me then and you've never stopped, dammit!" she exploded. "Let's face it, Ernest. You don't fucking love me. I gave my...ff-fucking heart to you and all these...ff-fucking years...you haven't changed!"

"Calm down, Janice. You're getting loud." Dad put his finger over her mouth. They both didn't realize that I was standing there listening.

"Don't try to *shush me,* biiiiitaaach! I was young and stupid before, but right now I am tired, Ernest. I really am. You have made my life a living hell. I'm tired of running. The only way I can cope with this shit is to get drunk. I am *tired of this God damned* Hennessey. I am tired of the lies. I am tired of yo' tired ass – "

"Baby," dad interrupted. "I'm sorry. I was really working this time, baby. I promise." Dad said it all with a straight face. I started to cry, and I couldn't stop crying. He was such a liar.

"I smell the liquor on your breath, muthfucka, and it ain't no cheap shit. I gets fuuucked up, remember, biiiaatch?" Mom began to cry uncontrollably.

"Look, dammit. I am telling you the fucking truth!" Dad got louder.

"Look who's loud now, buddy!" Mom stumbled and fell on the sofa.

"Look, I'm sorry. I just love you, baby, and I don't want to lose you. You and Lady mean the world to me." Dad pulled mom closer to him and started kissing her.

"I'm tired," mom cried quietly.

"Shhhh...." dad said as he started to slip off her pajamas.

"I'm tired..."

"Shhh, baby. I'm gonna make it alright..."

"I'm tir –"

I could hear my mother moaning. I couldn't look. I just went into shock right then and there. All those years, I had praised my father like he was the fucking King of Dads, and he had been lying to me the whole time. He actually sat there and lied to my mother, looking at her dead in her face, just like he had been lying to me all those years. All those years had been one big lie. All that time, I thought my mom was getting high because she was selfish. All those years I got on her, while dad just let me do it without saying a word. Who exactly *was* Ernest James Moore? **Who exactly was my daddy?**

"Did you enjoy yourself at Di Mimmo?" I said as I interrupted the abuse that my dad obviously called making love.

"Oh my goodness, Lady—" dad said and he and mom started pulling themselves together. They both wore a look of embarrassment.

"We had no idea you were awake," dad said, with his usual dumb, innocent tone.

"Yeah, and you had no idea I was at Di Mimmo's watching you kiss all over that fucking bitch while you were supposed to be at the office working late!" I screamed, as my dad smacked me so hard that he laid me out on the floor. My first reaction was to get up and start swinging. I lost my mind for a moment as mom stood between us, trying to calm us down. I was trying to throw punches at my father.

"Move, Janice. This girl done lost her fucking mind!" Dad pushed mom out of the way. I picked up the closest thing to me, which was one of mom's marble figures. I raised it at my father.

"All these fucking years and you lied to me!" I broke down crying with the statue figure still in my hand, in case dad tried to lay me out again.

"I hate you. I fucking hate you! You're a fucking liar! And if you come near me, I swear to God, I will fuck you up! You don't love us..." I began to tremble.

"You don't think I love you?" Dad's voice got weak. He was so hurt. You could tell by the look on his face.

"NO," I said.

Dad got a little teary eyed, turned around and walked away. He picked up his keys and just walked out the front door.

"Ernest," my mom said, trying to stop him. "Ernest!"

He just kept going. She looked at me and sunk into the sofa. She just stared at the wall and didn't move. I put the marble figure down and started to cry again. I just crumbled to the floor.

I'd never talked to my father like that. Parents in B-more would kill you before you got all up in their faces. That night was different. Dad was too wrong and embarrassed to do somethin'.

"Your dad loves you, Lady," said mom. "Sometimes, I think more than me. He is a good man."

Mom was taking up for him. I couldn't believe that shit. Was that how it had been all those years? One big cycle of abuse followed by a gang of lies? She kept looking at the wall. She knew the truth. She couldn't even look at me. I didn't say anything. I went upstairs to my room and picked up my cell phone to call John John.

"Yeah, John, can you come pick me up? I need to get out of here."

"You aight?" he asked.

"Can you just come pick me up now?"

"Yeah, I'm right around the corner at Dave's house. I'll be there in two minutes." John hung up.

I packed the rest of my stuff really quickly and ran downstairs. Mom was still sitting there, looking at the wall. She turned around when she heard me carrying my luggage. I could see John's lights from our window, so I went over to open the front door.

"Where are you going, Lady?" mom asked in a frantic tone.

"I love you, Mom. I know I haven't said it that much. I really do. But I'm leaving. I can't take another minute of this."

"How are you going to get to the airport? Your dad—"

"My what?!" I looked at her with so much hate that she couldn't even finish her sentence. She tried to get up to stop me but I was already taking my first set of bags to the truck. John started grabbing all of my bags that I placed at the door. Mom started to cry again as she tried to change my mind about leaving.

"You're a grown woman, Lady. Don't start your life off by running. You need to stay and work things out."

"I'm leaving, Mom, and that's it. I was leaving tomorrow anyway. I'll call you when I'm in L.A."

John was grabbing my last set of bags. I could tell he felt kind of awkward through all of it. I hugged my mother so tightly that I could almost feel her pain while she could feel mine. I turned around and I left. And I did not intend to set my foot back into our house again.

"You aight?" John asked as we rode in his truck.

I barely smiled. "Yeah."

"So, where do you want me to take you?"

"Your place."

"You sure?" he asked, looking at me intently.

"Yeah." I looked him dead in his eyes to let him know that this was not a game.

Chapter 5:
Who's Your Daddy?

We drove for about twenty minutes until we arrived in Owings Mills. The wind was blowing in my face as we drove in John's truck. The moon was almost full and I kept my eyes on it as it tried to hide behind the trees as we drove past. It was brighter than usual. We drove in silence the whole time. I could tell that he just didn't want to make it any weirder than it already was.

We pulled up to this development of phat condos and houses. All of the homes were new. When we arrived at the condos, all I could think of was how John John was doing it BIG for a young nigga in the game. I heard John was living kinda *aight* from Trina, and she wasn't lying.

I could hear the crickets making noise in the summer night. It had finally cooled down from a whole day of 95-degree heat. The humidity in B-more could make a nigga stay indoors until the sun went down. It was hot as hell!

It was like two o'clock in the morning by now, and I was exhausted. We left most of my bags in the truck so I would be ready to leave for

BWI Airport in the morning. We walked into John's condo and I was impressed—lil' John John had some class. He had a fireplace, flat screen TV, plush carpet, slate floors in the kitchen, modern furniture, and a balcony that stretched from his dining room to his bedroom. It was off the chain up in there. His house phone rang as I thought to myself that he had to have had all types of women up in his place. He excused himself to take the call in a room that he had turned into an office, insisting that the call was business. However, I knew that most of his business calls would have been taken care of on his Boost Mobile instead of his house phone. That was less likely to be traced. This call was definitely a booty call, but 'too late bitch' (whoever she may have been), I was already there. Being a virgin in B-more didn't necessarily mean you were naïve. I'd seen too much in my lifetime. In B-more, even a virgin had experience. I would let a nigga eat me out, I just wouldn't let a nigga hit.

I grabbed my stuff out of my bag so I could take a shower and went into his room. He had a king-sized bed with a Polo comforter and sheet set. He had his money just lying out on his dresser. He definitely wasn't expecting any company, because it was a stack of hundreds just sittin' out, chillin'. I was so sticky from earlier that I *had* to take a bath. I soaked in the water so long that my skin shriveled up.

After I go out, I slipped on my Donna Karen boy shorts and matching bra. John had the condo dimly lit. I could hear Usher playing in the other room. It was that really tight slow song that I liked.

"Lady!" John called from the other room. "You want anything to drink? Eat? I have Kool-Aid, water, apple juice…."

I walked into the kitchen in my underwear and John's mouth dropped so low to the ground that he looked retarded.

"Whoa now, Lady," he nervously said as he looked at me with the refrigerator wide open. I just stood there, looking at him. I began to talk to him with my eyes, and they were telling him that I wanted him. I was ready. He shut the refrigerator and walked over to me and began to kiss me slowly, almost cautiously. I kissed him back. He kissed me back harder. He pulled off his shirt and dropped it on the kitchen floor. He began to kiss me so hard that I started to moan. He picked me up and carried me to his room.

I watched him take his pants off and then his boxers. I looked at his penis in shock and thought, "Okay, I know *that* is not going inside of me!" He began to kiss all over me while he slipped off my boy shorts and then my bra. He looked at me one last time to see if I really wanted to go through with it and I shook my head "yes." He pulled out a condom from his nightstand, put it on and eased himself into me. It took a whole lot of minutes until he was able to get all the way in me, and when he did, I felt really uneasy. It felt good, but I felt kind of uncomfortable, and I knew it was a mess for him too. I began to cry and freak out, so he stopped.

"You okay? " he asked.

"Yeah." I looked away. I couldn't look at him.

"You've got to trust me, Lady. You've got to relax and just give yourself to me. Don't hold anything back, baby."

"I'm scared," I whispered. I still couldn't look at him.

"Of what? I'm your man. What's there to be afraid of?"

I looked at him and he was dead serious. He stroked my hair and began to kiss me again. He looked at me and said, "You're beautiful."

I kissed him back and wrapped my legs around him. He slid inside me again, slowly, and began to go deeper and deeper.

"Give it to me baby, give it to daddy...come on..." he said. The more and more he would tell me to give it to him, the more and more I felt myself letting go. I believed that I could completely let go without any fear. It was the safest that I had ever felt since I was a little girl.

When I was a little girl, I had felt so protected by my father. With everything going on at my house, John made me feel like I could be safe again. I didn't think that I would ever be able to feel safe again after I found out the truth about my dad. There I was, making love to John Anderson, and I felt like there was nothing in the world that could harm me—not even him. I started to feel really comfortable and I began to trust John. I felt like I could trust him with anything, including my heart. My eyes began to tear up and a tear rolled down my face. John looked at me, wiped my face and kissed me.

"Don't stop," I begged. "Don't stop..."

"You're beautiful, baby."

He went in deeper and deeper. He pushed himself into me almost in a way that told me he was marking his territory. He held me tightly and just kept holding me as he kept going deeper. I could feel my body letting down its resistance. The more he pushed his way in, the more I began to trust him, the more I wanted him to stay inside of me. It hurt so bad that it felt so good. I forgot about everything. All I could think about was giving myself to John--mind, body, and spirit.

"Who's your daddy?" he asked, as he went deeper and deeper into me. I began to feel all of the fear, hurt, brokenness, and sadness release from me for what felt like forever.

"You are." I agreed.

Chapter 6:
Cali Baby

"Yeah, I miss you too...you still coming this weekend to see me, right? Aight...can't wait to see you. Yeah. I'm okay. I don't want these L.A. niggas — I want you. Aight. Miss you too. Bye."

I hung up the phone wit' John John and put my cell back in my purse. I had to get myself under control. I just couldn't stop smiling.

I was standing outside of LAX, waiting for Trina to come and get me. I had never seen a palm tree in real life until that moment. It was tight.

Everyone was pulling up in a BMW, Benz, or any other luxury car that could come to mind. It seemed like everyone was tanned and wearing designer Shades. The airport was crazy busy. I wasn't even sure how Trina was going to be able to find me in all of the chaos.

I couldn't help but think about last night, and how I would never have guessed that I would lose my virginity to John John. I was kind of afraid, being that it happened so fast. I had definitely broken one of my mom's famous rules: *"wait at least three months to have sex, and if you do slip up, wait three more months before you do it again"*.

Well, I didn't plan on waiting that long. John was coming that next weekend and I was tryna *do it* again. He made me forget everything that had gone down with my folks. I really thought that I was falling in love with him. I just couldn't explain it. I mean, we are already together in a committed relationship. Plus, we had history. *Plus*, the nigga had offered to pay every last one of my bills: cell phone, rent, cable, groceries, and whatever else I needed. Not to mention he was getting me my first car when he came out to L.A. Momma didn't raise no mother fuckin' fool.

I was really starting to know what feeling sexy felt like. Even at the airport, all kinds of men were just staring at me - Black, White, Hispanic, and Asian...all races. I was used to niggas from B-more lookin', but at that moment I felt like a superstar up in that piece. Fuck dat! I felt like an international celebrity. I was super cute with my cargo shorts, tank top, beaded flip flops, and my favorite Gucci purse with matching Gucci glasses. I had to admit, since John and I slept together the night before, I'd discovered a part of me that I didn't even realize was there. Shit, Ma wasn't lyin' when she said that there was power in the pussy!

"What up, BITCH!!!" Trina yelled from the top of her lungs, pulling up in her Land Rover.

"Trinaaaa!!!!!!!" I yelled back. "Wassup nigga!"

Trina was my *dog*! She was super classy, as usual. I had to admit, L.A. had done her really well. She was a little thing, about 5'2". She had a cocoa complexion, the tiniest waist I'd ever seen, and as niggas in B-more would say, a *phat* ass. Her hair was always fly, and she always rocked a black silky weave. Whatever that girl had on, she ALWAYS worked the seams off of it. That day she had on a white wife beater with some Bermuda shorts. Ohhh, and she made me sick because she had on the Louis Vuitton flip-flops that I wanted with her matching Louis purse and Louis glasses. The girl was fierce. That was my best friend. We put the last bag into her Land Rover truck and we were off.

"Lady is *in* L.A.," she screamed. "Yeah, yeah!"

"Yeah, yeah!" I laughed.

"You look *good* ,girl."

"I *know* it," I said laughing.

"You still one cocky bitch." She rolled her eyes, smiling.

"Where did you get those shorts?" I asked.

"From this store called Fred Segal." She said. "So, you ready for the shoot? We're going straight to the set."

"Uh huh," I replied, in a nonchalant way. I was still thinking about the night before and how much I missed John already. He made me feel so special. Damn, I felt sexy. Shit, after last night, I knew I was! I began to smile thinking about how beautiful, sexy, and classy he said I was when we woke up that morning in his bed. I was still trippin' on how John John cooked breakfast for me.

"Lady, why are you glowing?" Trina started to pry.

"I am?" I said quickly. Dammit, Trina was on to something. She would never guess.

"You got some dick, didn't you? You dirty lil' hooker! You weren't even gonna tell me!"

"Huh?" I said quickly. How in the world did she know?

"You got some dick, Lady! Your lil' ass is glowing and you think you're the shit right now. Tell me, tramp!"

I smiled. Trina started laughing as she turned around to really look at me.

"*Who* was it!" she yelled and questioned. "Oh my GOD! Was it good? When!"

"No one," I lied. " I don't know what you're talking about."

"Tell it, bitch...as much dick as *I* get. I know what a bitch looks like after she just got laid."

I laughed. I had to admit, that was funny. Trina was so real that it was ridiculous. She was truly a trip. I couldn't even look Trina in her face. I knew she was looking at me, I could just feel it. I knew I had to tell her. She continued to pry.

"God don't like ugly. Who is it!?" Now she talked in an extremely serious tone.

"John."

"John John!?" she screamed. "Oh my God...are you serious?"

"Yeah."

Trina smirked. "I heard that nigga is packin, no offense..."

"*That's* none of your business, and I'm happy you don't know it for yourself. Let's keep it that way, aight?" I was firm, with attitude.

"*Damn* girl. He really put it *on* you. You *real* sensitive right now. Let me roll my window down, it's kinda HOT up in HERE!" She laughed. "Shit!" She kept laughing uncontrollably.

I laughed. I knew more questions were coming. It was just a matter of a half of a second. I could never keep anything to myself around Trina. She always had to know the "who, what, when, where, how, how come...."

"So when was this?" she predictably asked.

"Last night."

"Last night? Ooh, you lil' freak! Daammnn. Did y'all do it at his house? Is he really ballin' like I heard?"

"Yup. His place is phat."

"Was it good? He better had taken his time. Did it hurt?"

"Yeah, it hurt at first. It was good though." I smiled.

"Ewwwwww, you lil' freak! You smiling all hard and shit! Well, that's better than what I could say about my first time. Looking back, that nigga's dick was so little, he made my pinky finger look like the King of Dicks." She paused. "So...did you cum?"

"I don't know. I *think* I did."

"Nah, you ain't cum. You would know if you came or not, trust me." Trina grinned. "Miss tight ass Lady got her freak on last night. 'Bout time you got rid of those cobwebs in yo' pussy."

"At least my shit ain't stretched out!"

I laughed. Trina didn't.

"Whatever, bitch. So, wait—you just let him hit and that was it? You know, sex before marriage is okay, as long as you're *with* the person you're making love to or in love with. God honors those who try, and Lord knows I'm tryin' to find "the one"—tall, dark, packin' and PAID. I *know* Daddy Jesus wouldn't want it any other way. So, what, are y'all together now?"

"Yeah. He told me he was *all* about me, and that I better not talk to any of these L.A. niggas. He also told me to tell you that he would kick your ass if you had me out in the streets."

"Lil' John John can kiss my ass," she said without blinking. "He's all the way in B-more, whatever."

"He's coming to visit me almost every other weekend or so, *and* he's paying all of my bills."

"I knew I taught you well. That's right. God ain't gonna have you hooked up wit no broke ass nigga that can't do shit for you. Girl, play your cards right and you can have that nigga for life. Don't give him none when he comes to visit either. Make him wait."

I didn't really respond. "Oh…"

"Don't tell me your lil' ass is dick whipped already! *Girl*, you need to get control of your panties. You'd better learn how to sleep and roll. I'm telling you."

"Uh huh," I said, not really listening.

Rules were so dumb. John and I were already together. Why would I listen to Trina anyway? I had to admit, she always had control over every nigga she was wit'. She was a pro. She started having sex at twelve years old. She always seemed to have everything under control. She swore by going to church every Sunday. She said that the Lord kept her through the storms and all the heartbreaks. She did admit that she knew that having sex before marriage was wrong, but she said that God knew her heart. Trina would always say that she would ask the Lord to forgive her, but not having sex was just too hard. Besides, most of the people we knew didn't wait until they were married anyway. The only time Trina would ever feel guilty about having sex would be when she would slip up with someone she wasn't in a relationship with.

Trina was one of those women who *had to have it*. I'm not gonna lie, after being with John John, I didn't know why I had been holding out for so long anyway. I sure hoped John was my one and only, because I wouldn't know what to do. I definitely didn't want to stop having sex—not even for three months to honor some dumb rule.

"So let me tell you my good news," Trina smiled. "Lord Life has been *my man* for the past three months."

"What?"

"Yes, girl. He's been taking me on the road with him, buying me all kinds of expensive shit, paying my bills, and giving me an allowance...uh huh. I didn't tell anyone because I didn't want to jinx it. I even stopped talking to Chris Harris because of him."

"The NBA nigga? Are you crazy?"

"Lord Life is IT for me. We've been kickin' it almost every night and he got a nigga on lock. I don't mind it either...and he is so deep. You'll see, girl. He's really excited about meeting you."

Dang, Trina was doing it. She had options and shit.

Ring.

"That's Lord calling. He didn't pick up his phone one morning last weekend, so I've been ignoring his calls since then. He has been *on* me for the last five days. This nigga has called me at least ten times a day, and I haven't picked up the phone yet. Gotta train em'. These niggas are like dogs, Lady. Just watch and learn."

RRRing.

"You're not gonna get that?" I asked.

"Nope. He'll see me in a second. I want him to think it's over between us. Never nag a man about what he doesn't do, punish him with action. Men respond to strength. See, he will remember to pick up his mother fuckin' phone the next time I call. I don't care what time it is. You can train a nigga so well that he will take your call even while he is fucking another bitch. Train him right and he will put you first. Everything else to him will just be pussy."

Ring

Trina still wouldn't pick up the phone. Lord Life called her at least three more times, back to back. I looked at Trina with a look of disbelief. This sex thing was just way too complicated for me. Then I thought that maybe I *should* listen, being that she had the hottest rapper on her tip.

"See, Lady…" Trina continued "…men and women view sex differently. When men are in love, they can go to Bike Weekend in Florida and fuck another bitch and act like ain't nothing happen. It's just pussy to them. Sex is Sex. He's in love when he's spending his time *with* you and his money *on* you. He'll also do things like hang out with you instead of his boys. Women relate using mostly feelings, men don't. That's why when women cheat, men can't forgive. They know that it's more than just sex for us, even if we don't admit it. It tears their lil egos apart. "

I looked at Trina while she talked, tryin' to take everything in.

"Pussy is pussy for men. It's just a nut…*unless they run into some bomb ass pussy like mine!*" Trina laughed. "Even still, you have to know what you've got and make these niggas respect you. I really don't know if men even commit when they're married. Hell, I wonder 'bout that shit all the time. You even got preachers cheatin' on their wives. So, Lady, the lesson for today is 'Niggas ain't shit, so you might as well get some good dick and some money to pay for putting up wit' their sorry asses.'"

Trina was so spoiled. Her parents bought her everything she ever asked for. She'd been wearing designer clothes since she was in middle school. She definitely knew how to play the role in church too. She would have the whole church talkin' thing down-packed, and then she would come around us and kick it like she just wasn't in church on Sunday. Her dad was the reason why she was so spoiled. Since he was a pastor, his time was divided between his family and the church. He would just buy Trina and her mom things when he couldn't be there. Trina took that same attitude with the men she would be with. As long as they took care of home and bought her whatever she wanted, everything was okay. The only difference between Trina and her mom was that Trina didn't take no mess off of niggas. She was real quick to cut 'em if they didn't act right, no matter how much they would buy her. She would always say, *"A man will always do his dirt, but he'd better wash that shit off and leave the stank outside."*

"Aight, Diva," Trina said as she parked her truck. "We're here. Don't think you're gonna get out of telling me all about you and Mr. Anderson."

"Where are we?"

"On Sunset. We're shooting at the Viper Room for Lord's club scene. This is where you do your thang and show these bitches in L.A. who's really runnin' shit. I told him you could dance your ass off, so don't embarrass me."

"Bitch, please." I looked at Trina with confidence. "What's my name?"

"Lady…." Trina said, rolling her eyes and smiling.

"And where are we from?"

"B-more, bitch!" Trina yelled.

We both looked at each other and we knew what was next without saying a word. Trina put a CD in her player and it was B-more club music. She skipped the songs until we both heard:

"Out my way bitch – ahhhh!, Out my way bitch – ahhhh! Out my way bitch - ahhhh! Don't you see I'm tryna get through...."

The music blasted from her truck as we both hopped out and started dancing in the parking lot, out of control. It was like the old days back at the Paradox. We both laughed uncontrollably and gave each other five.

"Girl, I missed you," Trina said. "Let's go in there and rock this shit."

I had arrived. My first day in L.A. and I was already doing my first music video. My best friend was the lead actress and I was the lead dancer in the dance scene. I already knew I was going to get lead dancer, because I was the best.

We walked up from the parking lot and I saw three or four trailers parked off of Sunset Boulevard. Dang, this was really "for real." We walked past the first trailer and this handsome, dark chocolate piece of a man was standing outside next to it. As we walked closer, I realized that the man was Lord Life. Oh my goodness, it was Lord Life. I wasn't like star struck or anything, but I hadn't seen a celebrity that closely in real life. He looked taller on TV. He was like my height. He was still cute. He had his wife beater on with some jeans. He had that diamond studded Jesus piece and he was just cut all up. He looked at Trina as she and I walked right past him without saying a word. Trina didn't even look his way. She was so cold.

"Trina, let me talk to you for a second," he said in this voice that I'd never heard on TV. He always seemed like he was just extra hard. Trina had this nigga sounding like Tiny Tim.

Still walking she hollered back, "For what? You said all you had to say last weekend when you didn't pick up your phone."

Lord Life grabbed her and swung her around. She looked at him, rolled her eyes, and stood her ground to let him know that she wasn't playing. She snatched her arm away and put her hand on her hip.

"I'm listenin..."

"Baby, when you called me I was in a meeting with my manager. I couldn't pick up my phone, seriously."

"You think I was born fucking yesterday?" Trina said as she turned around to walk away. Lord Life grabbed her again. He pulled a small box out of his pocket and placed it in her hand.

"What the fuck is this? Oh, so I'm supposed to just suck your dick, because you went out and bought me something? I'm not for sale." Trina looked at him without blinking.

Lord Life opened the box and it was a princess cut engagement ring.

"I know you're not for sale, but will you marry me?" he asked.

Trina and I both were in shock. Our mouths dropped. I didn't know what Trina did to those niggas, but all of them was strung out on her coochie. This was like her third proposal in her lifetime. The first nigga who she *really* loved got locked up, and she gave the ring back to the second one when she moved to L.A., claiming that the ballers in B-more ain't have nothing on the ones in L.A. Now Lord Life, the hard-core player that every bitch in the world was in love with, was hooked! Trina looked at him with a straight face and he was serious. They had been dating for only six months and committed for like three months. Niggas back home in B-more used to always joke about how she had that good shit. It must've been, because she had the most thugged out nigga in the industry proposing to her and I was seeing it with my own two eyes. I could hardly believe it.

"Oh MY God....Yes! Yes!" Trina screamed. She grabbed him and kissed him. She turned around and winked at me while he slid the ring on her finger.

"AHHHHHHH....!" Trina and I looked at each other and both started screaming. Trina showed me her ring and we immediately went into 'girlfriend' mode. We acted almost as if Lord Life wasn't even there. You would have thought we were planning the wedding already.

"Uh-hum," Lord Life interrupted, "what's up, ma — you must be Lady. I've heard a lot about you, we gonna have to see you in action."

He shook my hand. "How about now?" I said with confidence.

"That's what I'm talkin' 'bout," Lord said. "Let's rock."

Lord grabbed Trina and pulled her close and began to kiss her again. I was so grossed out by then. After about two minutes of the excessive PDA (public display of affection), we headed inside.

We walked inside the Viper Room and Trina had that ring flashing every chance she got. We walked over to Lord Life's entourage and they all gave him dap and clowned him in a joking way about the engagement. They shook Trina's hand and Lord Life introduced me to everyone. The make up artist, who was kind of cute, practically ran over, interrupting the festivities.

"*Ohhhhhhh* my God, congratulations!" she said in one of those high-pitched, "white girl" voices that I thought only existed on T.V.

"Thanks," Trina said only to be polite. "Candy, this is Lady, she's the lead dancer for today's shoot."

"*Oh my goodness*...it's *so* nice to meet you!" Candy spoke, once again, in her perky, Beverly Hills voice. I looked at Trina to see if this chick was serious. Trina nodded "yes" and rolled her eyes.

"Likewise," I said calmly, almost laughing. I never thought that anyone would've been that excited for no reason in real life.

"Yeah! And you're soooo *cute* too." Candy further added to her embarrassment.

"Thanks."

Was I supposed to be ugly? She was weird. I was glad when she walked away.

"I hate that bitch." Trina whispered. "She is so phony, coming over here to congratulate me. Please, she was tryin' to fuck Lord Life at the last video shoot. You have to watch these hos."

Lord Life interrupted. "Scuse me, Lady. This is Shooky Simmons, the industry's top choreographer. This dude is hot. He's gonna run through part of the routine really quick."

"Okay," I said.

Shooky Simmons was obviously gay. Coming from B-more, you knew gay when you saw it. One of my good friends back in high school was gay.

He took me to the middle of the club to show me the combination. The club was small but it was tight, really grimy looking. There were about five main women dancers. I was the lead female dancer, (once I showed and proved.) We were doing the scene where Lord Life comes to the club and sees Trina's character in the middle of the dance floor. All of the dancers were supposed to be Trina's girls. She did light dancing while we rocked it in the back. His song, "Bang It" was about how he could put it down in the bedroom, *"Like a real thug supposed to."* (That was the catch phrase in the song.)

Shooky stood in front of me and did the entire combination. I watched closely, so I could lock it in and then add my own flavor to it. Once he finished, they played the music. It was a real hot, almost down south, dance beat. I could hear the music hit my bones with every bass drop. I hit every move and then added some of that B-more 'bout it' flavor to it. When I finished, everyone's face lit up.

Shooky Simmons came over and said, "*Okay*, I see you, mama."

I looked at Trina and she gave me the "wink" to tell me that I rocked that shit, even though everyone there was trying to play it cool. Wackos.

"All right, everyone", the director said. "Wardrobe, call time in an hour."

Trina and I went to Lord Life's trailer. We just sat around and cracked jokes. Lord Life rolled a blunt. Whatever weed he was smoking was strong hell. I started to catch contact in the first five seconds. Damn, it was nothing like the weed back in B-more. I would sit around niggas all day back home and I wouldn't catch contact. The trees that Lord Life was smokin' wasn't no joke. Everybody used to always say that Cali chronic was that real shit. They weren't lyin' either.

"You wanna hit?" Trina asked me as she took the blunt out of her mouth and slowly blew out smoke.

"I'm good."

"Aw c'mon — you bringin' minors around me, Trina?" Lord Life joked.

"Knock it off, aight?" Trina took up for me as she hit it again.

Trina and Lord Life took turns until the trailer was filled with smoke. I needed some air. I could never smoke weed or really drink like that.

I think growing up watching mom get fucked up on a daily just completely turned me of from even the thought of smoking weed and getting drunk. When they finished smoking, they started kissing all hard. I mean, didn't those idiots remember that I was there?

"I'm a go find my outfit for the shoot," I said. "I'll see y'all later." Those dummies kept kissing and didn't even respond to me. I already knew what was about to go down next. When niggas smoked, everything was just so predictable: first weed, then fuckin', then the munchies. Yep, they were gonna come out all hungry, smellin' like hot, funky sex. I was out.

Ring.

I pulled my cell out of my purse. It was John.

"Hey," I answered. "Yeah, I got the part. No, I'm not half naked. No, no niggas tried to get at me. Yeah, the dance number is off the chain. You miss me? I miss you too. Yeah, I can't wait to see you this weekend. Aight, I'm a call you later. Bye."

I smiled. I loved me some John Anderson right about then. All I could think about was how he talked, and that body...

"Hey, sexy," a man's voice said behind me. Who was this interrupting my joyous thought process? I did not feel like being bothered. What did that nigga want?

"What do you want?" I said, turning around to see who it was.

"If I told you what I wanted, would you give it to me?" he smirked.

The dude was wack. I thought, "Is this how men get at you in L.A.? " I looked closely into his face and realized he was that new R&B singer Tre' on Lord Life's label that sang the hook on "Bang It". His game was so tired. I didn't care how good this nigga looked. He was so wack.

"It depends on what it is…" I looked at him with a straight face.

"I don't want anything. But, what I *need* is your number."

"In that case, can't help you. Sorry."

I walked away. Did he really think I was going to give him the time of day with those rehearsed lines? Please, spare me. I did have to admit that he was kinda fine, though. Tre's complexion was like the color of toasted almonds. He was kinda short but he was muscular. He had a really clean cut and his eyes sort of slanted when he smiled. He had really broad features and nice full lips. He still wasn't as fine as John John.

I asked around until I found out where wardrobe was, so I could change into my outfit. Once I found it, I met up with the stylist. The lady was really stylish and pretty, with a short haircut. She had all kinds of clothes laid out. The outfit she picked for me was really cute. She pulled out some jean booty shorts and hooked it up with a really unique cream halter-top. I put on some large bamboo earrings and some bangin' stilettos to set it off.

Next, I had to go find Candy to do my make-up. I really wasn't excited about that part. I had a feeling that the chick was going to talk too much. I took my time looking for her until I finally ran into her, (and believe me, not on purpose.) I just happened to run into her on my way back to the club.

"Hey, sexy mama!" Candy exclaimed. Was she gay? Could she get off my clit? I spoke back.

"Hey, wassup,"

"I see you're ready for make-up. Your face is going to be fab...u...lous when I finish!"

I kept thinking she'd better not fuck up my shit. She was a little bit too excited for me. And what was up with the white girl voice? The bitch knew she was black. While Candy did her thang on my face, I looked around the club to observe all the people. The extras were called in and they were standing around getting directions from the director. As I checked out the guys, I was hoping that all of the guys in L.A. didn't look like what I saw in the club. Those flakes looked like they were all trying too hard. They were soooo wack. None of them could dress. They all looked like they attempted to achieve some pretty boy, hip-hop look. All of them had on jeans that actually fit - what kinda' gay shit was *that*? On the real, those niggas looked like Pretty Ricky's gone bad. Everyone there seemed to be going through a serious identity crisis.

And let me not get on the women! Every last chick there looked like she was going to be inducted into the next 'Queen of Hip Hop Videos

Hall of Fame'; none of them were that cute, all had weaves down to their butts, all of them wore hooker heels with extra tight jeans, and had perfectly fake boobs and lots of make up to hide the fact that their real faces were barking. Every dude looked like an R&B star wanna-be, none of them had their own personal style. It was so funny. I knew I stuck out in this cornball central. Those folks needed to get a grip on reality, quick! I couldn't lie, though—some of the females were on point. Made me feel like I needed to hit the gym or go get my eyebrows re-waxed or something.

"Wanna look?" Candy asked as she finished my face.

I grabbed the mirror from her and, to my surprise, she did my face up really tight. I looked extra fly. I had to give it to Miss Candy, she did her thang!

"It's tight, thanks." I said nonchalantly.

"Told you, FA...BU...LOUS!" she screeched.

She was cool up until that comment. *Did she really have to be that extra?* What exactly was she trying to prove? It was like she was doing a really awful job at trying to be cool. I guessed that was how those L.A. chicks did it. EXTRA.

"Aw, shit—somebody bout to do her 'thang-thang' on the dance floor!" Trina exclaimed out of nowhere. Just like I predicted, she came marching up with a bag of chips, a soda, some fruit, a granola bar, and a sandwich from catering. Back in the old days, after Trina would get fucked up at the club she would tear up a bag of plain Utz potato chips, some peanut chews, and a Pepsi Slurpee from 7-Eleven in the car on the way home. Then the heffa would convince me to go to Double T Diner with her at like three in the morning for some steak and eggs after she would really be coming down off of her high.

"Aight, out my way, rookie," Trina said as she pushed me out of Candy's chair. "The diva is next."

The Assistant Director started calling fifteen minutes until places as I walked around the club looking for Shooky Simmons. I finally ran into him next to the bathrooms. He took me out to the dance floor to go over the routine again. The shit was easy.

"I don't want you to lose that flavor you had earlier," Shooky said, really 'straight-to-the-point' like. "So, just get the steps down and then add your own shit. Aight?"

"Aight," I nodded.

Shooky went over the routine one more time as he hit every move, popping better than me. It was almost as if he had this imaginary phat ass instead of this scrawny little bootie on his backside. He made his ass jiggle better than I ever could make mine do, and I had way more than he did. He would take it all the way down to the ground and bring it back up again, hitting every bass drop with an ass drop and a chest pop. He was "gettin" it. I mean, this dude just hammered the song. I was going to have to work extra hard to hit it as hard as he did, and I had all the equipment naturally. But I wasn't worried because I was the shit.

Shooky stopped and looked at me to give the dance combination a try. He started the bridge of the song over again. I started dancing and went into this zone as I hit every move with conviction. I ain't gon' lie, the fact that I had just gotten some dick really helped me "feel" the song. The bridge played really loud in the speakers:

"Work it baby, work it. Twerk it baby, twerk it. I'm gon' crush and hurt it. Like a real thug suppose to. Drop yo' ass and hurt it. Bring it on up and turn it. Lord Life bangin' yeah, ya heard it. Like a real thug suppose to."

When I finished, bitches looked at me all hard. I knew I rocked it. Shooky and I were gonna be best friends.

Chapter 7:
You'd Better
Recognize

Music Playing.
> *"Lord Life bangin' yeah, ya heard it.*
> *Like a real thug suppose to."*

Trina and I drove in her truck, and I just kept thinking to myself, "I was in L.A.!" She pointed to an apartment building on our right side.

"This is where I stay, right there," Trina said casually.

The sign read "L'Estancia Apartments." There were mad palm trees and it was absolutely beautiful. I couldn't even put into words how 'off-the-chain' her apartments looked. My best friend was one classy bitch.

"This is *nice*, girl—what, what!" I exclaimed.

"What!" Trina replied.

We were so silly. We turned off of a street called Vineland and turned onto Ventura Boulevard. L.A. had the weirdest street names. Then we turned again on a side street to pull into her parking garage. Dang. It seemed like everything in L.A. was gated parking. I was gonna like this…

"What the fuck!" Trina yelled. "Who the fuck parked in my parking spot!"

There was a maroon colored, new Range Rover with mustard colored interior parked in her spot. I had to admit, I needed to see who was pushing it. It was bangin'.

"This is bullshit!" Trina yelled. "Whoever it is needs to move their shit. And they had the nerve to park the truck that *I* want in *my* spot. Ain't this some shit!" Trina was furious. She opened the car garage and slammed her foot in reverse.

We pulled up to the front of her building and I followed Trina as she jumped out of her truck. I didn't necessarily grow up in poverty, but all of the palm trees and crap had me feelin' like I wasn't used to anything. We walked into the marble floored lobby as I followed Trina to the manager's office.

"Hello, Trina." The manager greeted her. "Is everything okay?"

"Mrs. Robinson," Trina said in her extra professional "no-hint-of-I'm-from-the-ghetto" tone. "One of your tenants parked in my parking spot and I am really in a hurry. I need my parking spot cleared as soon as possible. Is there any way that you can tow the vehicle?"

"Not a problem," Mrs. Robinson smiled. "However, I don't think you would like me to tow your new truck before you got a chance to drive it."

Trina and I both gave each other a look of confusion. Huh?

"A Mister Lord Life told me you would come to the office to pick up your keys." Mrs. Robinson continued smiling.

Trina and I looked at each other and looked at the keys. We were both in a state of shock. When we finally came to, we smiled at each other.

"Thank you, Mrs. Robinson." Trina smiled and took the keys. "You have been most helpful, thank you so much." Trina winked at Mrs. Robinson and Mrs. Robinson winked back.

Trina and I practically ran through the halls to the parking garage entry. When we got to the parking lot, we both just screamed. Trina opened the new maroon colored Range Rover with mustard colored interior. She turned the engine on and what sounded like a Lord Life song that had not been released yet was blaring out of the truck's speakers. It was a real tight hard-core beat, with Lord Life half singing the hook:

Music Playing.
"Shorty, you can take the keys to my
Range. Shorty, you ride hard for a
nigga in the game.
Shorty, I wanna see a smile on your
face. Shorty, yeah you're my
shorty..."

We screamed as we bugged out in the front seat. It was unreal. We screamed again. I had to give it to Trina once again—she was the *truth*!

"Awwwww, thank you, babe!" Trina squealed as she talked on her cell. She had to be talking to Lord Life. "I was so surprised! *Oh yeah.* Yeah, you can see mama tonight. I'm a take care of you."

Trina smiled all hard. I knew what that meant—I wouldn't be seein' Trina that night. She was 'bout to further pussy whip that nigga into buying her a house, a jet, or some shit. Keep playin'!

"Aight, girl," I said jokingly. "So when you gonna school me on how to get John John to buy me that Lexus truck I want?"

"Girl," Trina said, rolling her eyes. "I've been trying to tell you how. Your lil' dick whipped butt won't listen to me."

"I'm *all* ears."

I was serious. I wasn't planning on using everything she told me. I think I really loved John John. Besides, all those games weren't me. But it didn't hurt for me to get a couple of pointers, especially from a woman who'd just gotten engaged to the hardest nigga in the rap game. Not to mention, he had just gone all soft and pulled a Love Jones move on her by surprising her with a new Range Rover.

"I'm listening…" I said.

▪▪

We pulled up to the Aqua Nightclub in Beverly Hills in the new Range. We were shittin' on every chick in front, inside, on her way to, *and* leaving the club. WHAT? That evening was Lord Life's album release party. Even though Lord Life was all thugged out, he was a strategic businessman. He was very classy, not your average thug. I noticed that everything in L.A. was valet parking. It was fucking sick! I LOVED L.A.!

"Check my back, can you see my thong?" Trina asked. She wore her extra low ride pants with a top that had most of her back out. She was nowhere near hoochie, either. Trina had a unique way of making the hoochiest of clothes look really classy.

"No, you're straight," I said while we walked up to the club.

"Aight, girl." Trina grinned. "You ready? You look fly, mama!"

"I *know* that's right," I said with assurance. I had on my white, almost see through H&M top, (I was on a stylish budget that night), my extra tight khaki colored club pants, my Jimmy Choo coffee colored four inch pumps, and my hair was swept up into a sexy bun. We walked past the line and stood in front of the guy who was checking names. He was a cute lil'cocoa thang.

"What's your name?" he asked.

"Trina Parker," Trina said in her professional tone.

"Alright, Ms. Parker plus one. Here are your wristbands." He put bright yellow bands on our wrists. "The VIP section is straight back and to the right, next to the bar."

"Thanks," I said and smiled.

"You're welcome, sexy." He smiled extra hard, winking at me. Wow. The dudes I kept running into had no game. NONE. I hope every man in L.A. wasn't like that.

The Aqua Nightclub was nice, really classy. Clubs in Baltimore were okay, the ones in DC were nice, but this club was *nice*. As soon as we walked in the club, I could here Lord Life's album playing. The party was supposed to be really exclusive, and it sure looked like it to me. Trina told me that there were going to be a lot of record execs and other people in the entertainment industry there. Those people *looked* like they had money. They had girls wearing some super tight t-shirts, passing out samples of liquor. They really looked like they were trying entirely too hard. I swear I saw one girls' entire nipple print. Wow.

We walked past the guard and walked into this really small VIP room. Lord Life was sitting there with his entourage. His face lit completely up when he saw us.

"There's wifey," he smiled.

Trina flashed her ring all around and went over to kiss him. They practically swallowed each other's tongues; they were so nasty. All of the PDA was so not cute.

Lord Life called out, "Hey waiter, bring me a bottle of —"

"Babe, " Trina interrupted, "I'm not feelin' that boogie shit right now. Just gimme a double shot of Henney, and Coke on the side to chase it."

Lord had this really surprised look on his face. I had to admit, Trina was not playing that night.

Trina leaned into Lord Life seductively. "I'm getting ready for our private party tonight," she whispered.

"Whatever the lady says, bring her what she wants," he said proudly. He looked like he could have just busted a nut right there in the middle of the club.

"Lady, what you want?" Lord Life asked, looking at me.

"I'll take a ginger ale," I said.

"Naw, bring her an Apple Martini," Lord interjected. "Are you sure you're over twenty-one? How old are you, twelve?" He laughed.

I knew this Negro wasn't just trying to embarrass me in front of all those people. I didn't care if he thought he was the shit. *No one* embarrassed *me*.

"No, but I'm old enough to order my *own shit*," I said, staring at Lord Life without blinking. "Waiter, bring me a ginger ale. Thank you." I rolled my eyes.

"Damnnnnnnnnnn!" Lord Life's boys said, sounding like a bunch of echoes.

"What!" Lord Life laughed, along with all of his boys. "We got a rider up in here. You ain't Trina's best friend for nothing. I see you — you can dance *and* put a nigga in his place. You cool wit' me."

I smiled and rolled my eyes once again. **They'd better recognize**. I was from B-more and we didn't play those L.A. "kiss-your-ass" games. We kept it real.

Everyone's eyes were on us. Being that we were with Lord Life and his crew, we turned into instant celebrities. The women were looking at us so hard that I felt like I'd made a wrong turn into lesbian night at The Paradox back in B-More. People were so "eager" in this city. *Dang.*

Then, Lord Life spoke up. "Ladies, this is Hank Thomas. He's the best A&R man in the country. He makes shit happen on my record label."

"The pleasure is mine, ladies." He kissed our hands. He was handsome for a white boy. He had me looking at him harder than how I looked at the brothers. He was *fine*. He had this almost golden complexion and blonde hair cut really close. It almost looked as if he had a shape up like a black dude. His build was stocky like a football player. I swear I saw every curve of his muscles in his button down shirt.

"What it do!" said Tre', appearing and interrupting my life again. I thought he was from Philly and not L.A. He was really busted, going around saying *"what it do"*.

"What's good," Lord Life responded. "Tre', you know Trina. And this is her best friend, Lady. She just moved here from Baltimore."

"Yeah, we've met," Tre' said nonchalantly. "Track number three on the album is the truth. That new producer Rob Man got beats for days. That dude is tough."

Tre' was obviously making a point that he was not that interested in Lord's introduction to me. He was such a jerk. Wacko.

Music Playing.
"Niggas wanna act tough, but they
don't wanna see me. I don't have to
say much, I'm a real motherfuckin G."

"Yo, that's my *shiiiiit*!!!!" Trina yelled at the top of her lungs when she heard Lord Life's song. She turned to Lord Life. "We'll be right back, babe."

"I love that girl," Lord Life said as we ran off into the crowd. I could hear his boys clowning him as we left. The super hard, thug ass nigga Lord Life was whipped, and I was there to see the shit for myself.

"Peep game, girl," Trina said in my ear when we were away from Lord Life and his boys. "Remember when I stopped him from ordering the expensive shit and I told him I only wanted Henney and Coke?"

"Yeah, talk a lil' louder, yo." I was raising my voice above the music.

"Aight. That shit was subliminal. I wanted to show him how much I appreciated him. Any other bitch would have just kept going and had him order the fancy shit. The Hennessey and Coke remind him of something his best friend might order."

"Okay and your point?" I said.

"That one simple thing sets me apart from any other bitch he's ever had in his life. Living life is about choices. I choose to be cheap in the small stuff, so he'll want to spend more on the big stuff." Trina had a look of arrogance like I'd never seen before.

"I don't get it," I said. Really, what *was* her point?

"I stroked his ego by ordering cheap shit. I let him know that I cannot be bought without even saying it. He's trying to buy me all this shit to own me. That's what men do when they are in love."

"Uh-huh," I said, starting to kind of see her point.

"Just like his best friend, I'm gonna be there. Just like good old Hennessey and Coke. I am not the latest new shit that eventually goes out of style; I ain't goin' nowhere. I'm what you get drunk off of. You feel me?!"

"I think." I kept thinking. "Ohhhhh! The average person doesn't get drunk off of that expensive shit."

"Right! Men are like computers. They respond to action. That's my lesson for the day." Trina smiled approvingly. "Don't get me wrong. I love him, but you can't ever let these niggas think they know you. They get bored."

"Niggas never get tired of Hennessey," I said, realizing her point.

"Exactly," she said knowingly.

Trina wasn't no joke.

Chapter 8:
Feelin' It

I couldn't believe it was 7a.m. Even though we hadn't left the club and gotten home until 3a.m., I popped right up like it was one in the afternoon. The time difference was a trip. It was like 10am in B-more. I really was in L.A....

I had only been there for less than a week and I was the shit. I had gone to the hottest industry party on the freakin' planet *and* I had booked a video. It was unreal. Bitches had been out there for years and they still couldn't top my grind. Shooky Simmons, the hottest choreographer in the nation, already told me that he was going to book me for all his major shit: videos, award shows, concerts, the list went on. I knew it was only the beginning.

I rested in Trina's bed and couldn't help but think about how everything was moving so fast. I really didn't want to get out of the bed yet. I swear—Trina had the most comfortable bed ever. The bitch had class. She had tan, cream, and brown Ralph Lauren sheets with a matching down comforter. It felt like I was sleeping at the Regency Hotel on Park Avenue in New York. Her throw pillows were cream and tan lamb suede. Can somebody say soft? The cream satin pillowcases blended right in.   Her duvet cover was pure linen with satin binding. She had pink flowers on her night stand to accent everything. Her area rug next to her bed made your feet feel like you were walking on a cloud. That thang was plush.

Her entire apartment looked like something off of MTV cribs. She had that fresh, traditional, modern look down. The curtains in her bedroom were this really pretty coffee and pink pattern to pick up the gold and cream stripped chaise by her window. Everything was so classy and modern with a nostalgic type feel. She made me so sick with her sepia colored pictures of herself accenting her walls all around her room. It was really pretty up in there. I couldn't wait until John John came out, so I could get my apartment hooked up.

I was kinda happy that Trina didn't come home to sleep after the club, because I took full advantage of her cozy bed. A lot had gone on in a little bit of time since I'd arrived in L.A. Finding out all that stuff about my dad really hurt me like hell. And to think, I had been saving my virginity until I was married because my dad talked about how a true lady should wait. After that episode he pulled, I didn't believe anything he had told me. Besides, giving it up to John John was the best thing I'd ever done.

Ring.

"Hey, you," I said, smiling all hard. It was John John. "I was just thinking about you."

"Good, you ready to see me?" he said.

"I miss you like hell," I said without hesitation.

"I'm on my way."

"Stop playin," I said, smiling. John John played too much.

"For real," he said seriously. I just rented me a Dodge Magnum and I'm on the 405."

"Yo, how did you know how to get to the 405?" I said, surprised.

"Trina lives in the valley, right?"

"Yeah."

"Okay, I asked shorty at the gas station, and he told me to get on the 405 north." John's tone shifted. "Why—you out here fucking some other nigga? You act like you not tryna *see* me."

"Naw, yo. I'm just surprised. I can't wait to see you." John was acting all weird.

"Aight. We'll see when I get there. Ask Trina how I get there from the 405."

"She ain't here. Hold on, I'm a call her."

Wow. John was not playing. I hadn't expected him to come out for two more days. He just up and got on a plane and just popped up in LA. John was way past gangsta. *Wow.* But he was also trippin', constantly asking me if I was interested in other niggas. What was his problem?

■■■

John John was in LA and had put down a deposit and paid my first month's rent for me to live at L'Estancia with Trina. I got my keys and everything. Just when I thought that L.A. couldn't get any better, John put the icing, the decorations, and the candle on the cake. Since he arrived, it'd been part two of the "Lifestyles of the Ghetto Fabulous." A bitch was lovin' it!

The next day we rode around getting furniture and everything for my apartment. I was able to get the bedroom set I really wanted from The Pottery Barn. I got all types of accessories from Crate and Barrel, and I got my living room and dining room set from Plummers on Venice Blvd. My living room furniture was the cutest retro pieces that I'd ever seen. I picked out a cream leather sofa with a matching ottoman. John John told me that I could pick out whatever I wanted, no matter the cost. I was impressed.

Later, we walked up and down Melrose and he bought all kinds of clothes for the both of us. I went fucking crazy! Melrose was real cool and had some really good accent pieces for my wardrobe. Actually, Melrose was kinda fabulous. The shops were really trendy, and I found all kinds of unique items. A lot of people hung out there on the weekends. We walked past these biker boys and John almost lost his mind making sure none of them looked at me when we walked past. He was so serious that he made it a point to put his hand on my butt as we walked by. Then, we drove further down the street and shopped some more at Ron Herman.

The day after, John took me to Beverly Hills and I got this Fendi bag I really wanted. Beverly Hills was crazy! There were silver street signs, silver fire hydrants, and a pedestrian walkway in the street that crossed diagonally from one corner to the next in front of the Louis Vuitton store. I guess when you have money practically coming out yo' ass, you start inventing rules. I'd never seen a diagonal crosswalk ever in my life.

We then went to Anastasia's and I got my eyebrows done while John got a facial. Trina went there all the time to get her eyebrows and her facials done, so she scheduled our appointment with her regular person. We had a late lunch at Crustaceans a couple of blocks away, and ordered this humongous crab entrée that was off the hook. They took the crab meat out the shell and seasoned it. It was off the chain. The bill was like three hundred dollars, damn! I was used to eating good, but DAMN!

Just when I thought it couldn't get any mo' better, John surprised me by taking me to the Lexus dealer and bought me the truck I wanted: a new, fully-loaded Millennium Silver Metallic Lexus RX 350 with black interior. He told me that Trina set everything up with the dealer. She was a true best friend.

So in a matter of days, I had a new fully furnished apartment that looked like something off of HGTV, more clothes that I could event count, and a new luxury truck. I couldn't wait until all of my furniture arrived. I was going to decorate my butt off.

We had to spread out on my living room floor with my new Armani bedding set. My bed wasn't arriving until the next day and John had to pay extra to get them to rush it. He insisted that they deliver it early because he didn't want me sleeping on the floor like some project bitch.

My apartment was huge. I couldn't wait until I got my stainless steel refrigerator. We laid out on the floor and ate strawberries and whipped cream in my new apartment.

"Lady," John said, looking as if he'd been contemplating something.

"What's up?" I continued to look at him.

I laid on his chest as he stroked my hair. Resting in his arms was the best feeling I'd ever felt. John was the type of man that made you feel protected at all times. Even though he didn't play when it came to business and the streets, he had this soft side that I'd been seeing a lot of lately. His eyes were almost glowing while he was thinking of what to say.

"I'm gonna be here a lot more," he said quickly.

"For real?" I was almost jumping out of his arms.

"Yeah. I've been doing some research and I can do some big things out here. You know, maybe open up a high-class barber and beauty shop. I can be bi-coastal."

"Okay..." I said, surprised.

"I'll just live here with you and then keep my condo back east. If things go really well then I can just turn my property back east into some income property." John continued to think.

"What about the barber shop and promoting parties?" I asked in disbelief.

"Man, that's small shit. I 'm tryna do *big* things. I really wanna get out the game, and I can make more money here. Niggas out here living nice just selling weed - "

I cut John off with my look of disapproval. I knew he wasn't thinking about coming to L.A. to do his thang-thang. He was almost fully out the game back in B-more. I was really not tryna deal with all of that extra drug shit at that moment. I did not move to L.A. to be the star of "The Wire: The Cali Edition".

"Babe," he continued, "I'm not gonna do what you're thinking. I got enough money saved up all over the place so I can open up my shop in about a month. Plus, don't you need a manager to keep all these niggas from thinking they gon' get some?" John caressed my breast, looked at me and kissed me on my lips softly. There went me holding back sex for three months, because I was not about to tell him to stop.

Everything was moving so fast that it almost seemed like it wasn't real. In a week I had a new apartment, and new truck, a new career, and a new man who was about to drop everything to come live with me. I knew John was going to pay of all my bills for the most part, but he was actually trying to build something with me. I was going to be the hottest dancer out there and after that I could pretty much do whatever I wanted: movies, commercials, and TV. That's how a lot of people got started. John was actually talking about being my manager, and he had the business sense to do it. He was the only one I would trust out in L.A. anyway, besides Trina.

It almost seemed like John was trying to marry me sometime soon. I'd never heard of him doing everything he did for me for *any* woman before. I wasn't trying to rush anything, because everything was so new. All I wanted to do was to live in the moment. And right then, I was getting my pussy ate. I wasn't trying to think about anything else but the fact that if there was a heaven on earth, then *this* must be it. Any heffa would've wanted my life right then.

I was feelin' it.

Chapter 9:
Don't Knock
My Hustle

"Church was off the hook," Trina said as we left Faithful Central. "Man, Bishop Ulmer can teach!"

Trina's church was huge. It was like the size of a football stadium. Trina told me that the Lakers used to play there. I really didn't like huge churches, but this one was different. The Pastor did break the message down. I really didn't feel like going to church, but the messages were different. I actually could understand what the pastor was talking about. Usually when I went to church, the pastor was so busy running around screaming on the microphone that I didn't even know what he was saying. He actually broke everything apart, explained everything and then brought everything back together so that it made sense. I actually broke down and cried at the end.

"You should come every week," Trina said, all excited. "It's off the hook, I'm telling you!"

"We'll see," I said, almost avoiding the question. It was good and all, but I didn't know about going every Sunday. I loved God, but I really didn't think that going to church every Sunday was going to get me into heaven. There were a lot of people, (for instance, Trina), who went to church every Sunday, and I didn't see how *they* were different than anyone else. Trina went almost every Sunday and got dick almost every Saturday night before Sunday service. Knowing Trina, she at least had to "get some" five out of seven days of the week. She acted like a nigga. I wasn't gonna lie, since my encounter with "getting it", I didn't see me going on strike any time soon. Between the D-I-C-K and getting licked every night, I was real content.

Trina would smoke weed while quoting Bible scriptures. It was ridiculous. It was like every time she smoked, she got real spiritual and shit...like I was supposed to listen to her ramble on and on about how Jesus saves while she was high.

I knew the basic things: NO sex before marriage, NO drinking, NO cursing, NO lying, NO stealing, NO fun, blah, blah, blah. What was I supposed to be? A fucking nun? I knew them bitches be playing wit' their clits while no one was looking.

Every time I even picked up the Bible on my own, I fell asleep. Besides, every time I even thought of getting closer to God, all kinds of weird shit started happening. I couldn't even read the parts in the Bible when they talked about Jesus casting out demons and all that other craziness. Every time I read those parts I would start to get really cold and I would start shaking. It would feel like I was outside in zero degree weather even though it would be hot outside. I was *cool* on church. Trina would tell me how she would "see" things sometimes. She said that as soon as she would say, "The blood of Jesus", those things would disappear.

Plus, I didn't know if I even believed everything in the Bible anyway. Regular men wrote it, so how did I know they didn't slip anything extra in it?

All I knew was that everything was fine as long I didn't start picking up the Bible and thinking about going to church. Obviously, God had something else better for me to do besides communing with the fake church folk. Besides, I prayed every day and I knew God answered my prayers. I knew God was real. I just didn't know if Church and the "Church folk" were real. I really didn't understand the whole Jesus thing. How was Jesus God? No one could seem to break that down for me. I wasn't saying it was a lie. I just wasn't going to believe in something that I didn't understand just because it was the popular thing to do. So I just stayed as far away from church as I could. I just made sure I prayed everyday.

Don't get me wrong, I loved God. I really did.

Chapter 10:
The Business

It had been eight months since John John first opened his barber/beauty shop "New Images", and business was off the chain. John decided that its location should be in Studio City so that it would be a convenient drive for everyone who lived in the valley.

I was consistently dancing, and now I was a local celebrity. Being a local celeb in L.A. really meant that people all over the country recognized you from the videos and the awards shows, but you were still just another person among the crowd as far as L.A. was concerned. I was still gaining niggas' respect. I was booking every video imaginable and I even did the AET, NTV, and Vibration Music Awards. John John was my manager.

Trina and Lord Life were still engaged, and they were planning for their wedding to happen in about a year. They decided to wait that long so he could be done with the tour that he was preparing for. Their wedding was the talk of the valley. Everyone was still in shock that Lord Life was getting married.

I opened the door to John's shop. I had just come back from being on the road, dancing for an artist on tour. Business at the shop was good as usual. John had the natural ability to run a business. He also had the marketing skills of someone who could work at a million dollar corporation. He was smarter than most.

The shop was medium-sized, located in a shopping center. On the side of the shop for the women, the walls were painted a light purple. The stations for the hairdressers were cherry wood tables with light gold mirrors over top. Each one had an orchid flower as an accent piece. Instead of using the standard chairs for the hair dryers, John used a really modern looking sofa. You could almost fall asleep while waiting for your hair to dry. There was also some pretty sheer white fabric draped over the top of the ceiling near the ladies' bathroom. On the side for the males, the walls were painted cream. The stations where the men got their hair cut were black modern looking tables with silver knobs. There were black and white pictures of different sports legends and celebrities hung on the wall to bring out the "black and white" theme. As soon as you walked in, there was a really pretty cream sofa on the right and the same cream sofa on the left. I helped John with all of the decorations. It was real classy.

John was a genius. He didn't close off the men's and the women's sections. This caused the shop to be known as the number one social spot next to a club in the valley. Almost half of the celebrity community came to the shop to get serviced.   I looked forward to going to the shop, especially when the comedians stopped by. You were guaranteed to see a free stand up comedy show right there in the shop. If you wanted to see the girls in the videos, you could see them at New Image. They came for two reasons: a killer weave and to get their rent paid. Yes, every baller imaginable got his hair cut at John John's shop. They ranged from thugs to sports players, to superstars. Plus, it helped that Lord Life rapped about New Image on a new song from his upcoming album.

I ran straight to the ladies' room as soon as I set foot in the shop. Coming off of early evening traffic on the 101 was no joke.

"Hey, girls," I said, walking past the beauticians on my way to the bathroom. Everyone said "hi" back in unison.

"Stacey," I said quickly, to my favorite stylist. Stacey could do hair like my momma.

"Yeah, boo," she said.

"Where's John John?"

"He went to get something to eat."

"Aight."

I had to pee so bad. As soon as I walked out of the bathroom, I saw John John through the shop's glass windows in the front, talking to this white girl named Emily that was on every video set swearing she was black. She was infamous in the rap game for her "tricks."   I could feel everyone's eyes on me as I walked to the front to go outside.

"Hey, sweetheart," he said as he saw me opening the front door.

"Hey," I said softly as I rolled my eyes. John had lost his mind. It's like this nigga was trippin off this L.A. shit. Niggas came to L.A. and lost their minds.

"Byeee, John, " the white girl practically sang as she walked away to her car.

"Byeee, biiiaaatch," I sung back to her, rolling my eyes. Then I turned to John.

"What the fuck you doin' talking to that white devil," I asked loudly, so she could hear me.

The white girl Emily rolled her eyes when she heard me, then she smiled. Wrong move, never smile at an angry *black* woman.

"Keep walking, ho, befo' I slap that silly smirk off yo' mutha fuckin' face," I said quickly. She kept walking and rolled her eyes as her smile disappeared.

"Trailer park bitch!" I said, loud enough for her to hear again.

I looked at John and he had a smirk on his face. He had really lost his mind. That did it—I was officially angry.

"What the fuck you smiling for?" I asked with a stern I'm-not-playin'-games attitude. "You've been actin' real brand new, John. I don't know if –"

"You know you real cute when you mad, babe," John said smiling.

"I don't have time for your games, John. What the fuck was that?"

"She stopped me on my way into the shop and asked me if there were any 'walk-ins' today." John talked with a straight face, looking at me in the eyes. He must've really thought I was real stupid.

"Your game is really getting wack with that one, you can do better than that shit. So you both happened to be pulling up at the same time? She asking you 'bout a walk-in…like you do hair."

"Babe, I *own* the shop," John said as he kissed me on my cheek close to my ear. "Chill out, for real—you know you're my lil' momma. I left to go buy you this from the mall up the street."

John went to the front seat of his new Black 7 series BMW parked in front of us and pulled out a bag from Victoria's Secret. I peeked in it and saw this really pretty lingerie from the tabbed page in my Vicky's magazine at our house in the bathroom. I circled it so I could remember to order it. I couldn't help but to blush.

"Uh-huh, you know daddy gone take care of you tonight," John said as he smiled with those dimples. "My baby all frustrated, I know you miss me."

"You get on my nerves, yo."

"That's why you smiling. You know I be wearing that fine ass of yours out."

"Is that right?" I said, grinning hard. I couldn't lie. Sex with John John was *real* good those days. I definitely knew what an orgasm felt like. Trina wasn't lying when she said that I would know when I had one.

"Uh-huh," John said as he kissed me gently on the lips.

"Ummmmmm...yo, John." One of John's barbers from B-more who worked in the salon interrupted, leaning out of the front door. "Big Mike is on the phone about some hair products."

"Aight," John said quickly. "Tell him I'll holla at him later. I ain't forget about him."

"John," I whispered angrily. "I know you not still doing your thang thang. Why is Mike calling you? I know it ain't for no hair products."

"Look, Lady. I'm not discussing this right now."

"Aight, John. Whatever." I started walking away to go back into the shop.

"Lady, I'm just trying to take care of us. Plus, I can't be having my baby lookin' like she aint' no celebrity. I'm your man and your manager. I take care of us. How I get things done around here is none of your business, aight?"

"Like I said, whatever." I walked away without even looking at him. I was fed up. John John had been talking about how he was going to give up hustlin' for a while. It seemed like the more money he made, the more he kept hustlin'. Niggas got real greedy out in L.A.

I walked inside the shop and John John followed behind me. I could tell that everyone was being nosy and had been looking at us through the windows during the whole incident.

I really tried to hide the fact that I was bothered by John's metamorphosis into becoming one of the most sought after niggas in the valley.

Almost every woman wanted him. He was officially "The Pussy's Most Wanted." He was like a local celebrity now too. Black, White, Chinese, it didn't matter. In L.A., the color was green. John not only had the money, but he also had the charm and the looks. Not to mention he was instantly a celebrity once everyone saw him hangin' with Lord Life and his crew. Everyone knew it was just a matter of time before he started his own management company. He was already known as my manager, and he had started doing some things for Lord Life's R&B act Tre' as his road manager. Women in L.A. were so hungry that it was ridiculous. You could be butt ugly; but if you were a sports player, actor, singer, rapper, or anything else that would grant you celebrity status, then you were all of a sudden "*fine*." Please, I knew half those niggas wouldn't get no ass if they were just some regular broke down nigga on the street.

Plus, there was something about a man from the east coast that was different from any man from anywhere else. A man from the east coast could turn heads just wearing a white T, jeans, sneakers, and a nice watch. It was all in his swagger.

I sat in the waiting area until Stacey called me for my appointment. Stacey was a really stylish light skinned woman. She always rocked the best weaves, and she had natural style. Even though she didn't always wear the latest designer clothes, you couldn't tell. She was one of those women who could make anything look good. She wasn't petite but she had the cutest figure. She was thick all around, but everything was proportioned evenly. She also had the prettiest eyes that almost seemed to glow when you would look at her. I think she told me she was in her mid-twenties, but she always seemed to act older, in my opinion.

I was definitely not gay, but there were many times when I would sit in admiration of how Stacey dressed and carried herself. Not only was she pretty, but she was comfortable in her own skin. Anyone who met her could tell that she was different from most women. She was one of the coolest women I knew, even though I wouldn't tell her that to her face.

John John looked at me from across the room and smiled. I couldn't help but to smile, but I couldn't lie. I knew that John was my first and we lived together and he took care of me financially, but something deep down inside didn't seem right anymore. I couldn't put my finger on it. I would see him entertaining his little pool of groupies, but I couldn't say that he was cheatin'. No one ever called the house, his cell, the shop, and everyone knew I was his woman. I could see the look of jealousy in women's faces when John would drop everything to cater to me whenever I came around.

"Alright, c'mon Miss Thang," Stacey said in her usually happy tone.

"Hey, girl," I said, smiling to hide the fact that I was uneasy.

"You want the usual?" she asked.

"Yeah," I said, still in deep thought.

"Girl, smile! You too pretty to be all frowned up." Stacey said this with a smile so real that I couldn't help but smile back.

"Hey, Stacey," Gino the comedian interrupted.

"Hey, Gino," Stacey said back, still smiling. "What's goin' on?"

"Stacey, now you know you too fine to be holding all that good stuff you got hostage. What you *waitin'* for?" Gino talked in a sarcastic way, loud enough for the entire female side of the salon to hear.

"I'm waiting for the Lord...and for you to get out of my face wit all that mess!" She put him in his place. "I still love you though, boo."

"*I'm tellin' you*. You *need* to stop runnin all these niggas away with all that Jesus talk! Why can't you be like *everyone* else and just go to church on Sunday and be a ho during the week? Y'all know y'all be shoutin' on Sunday and ho'in' Monday through Saturday. I be seein' some of y'all at the club, givin' it up on the dance floor! What you call 'dat? Shakin it fo' Jesus? *'I'm just shakin' it fo' Jesus!'*" He said dancing, mocking how women dance at the club. "Y'all know what I'm talkin' 'bout. Then y'all be gettin' re-saved on Sunday!"

Gino was on a roll and had everyone else laughing with him. I was glad he said it, because I sure was thinking it.

"Boy, shut up!" Stacey said, laughing just a little bit. "It's a lifestyle, Gino." "Being saved is a

Sunday through Saturday thang." She broke it down while she worked the perm in my head.

"And you 'bout the only woman up in here who's *savin' it*." Gino continued.

"Boy, go somewhere and sit down before you get struck by lightening. You know God don't like ugly, talking all that mess."

"You know you *want* me, Stacey," Gino said confidently. "Admit it."

"You need Jesus, boo."

"There we go. I'm done here. You done brought Jesus up. See what I'm talkin' bout?"

Gino walked away, still cuttin' up, laughin'. Stacey had finished working my perm in and she took me to the bowl to rinse my hair out. Episodes like the one that happened with Gino and Stacey were regular scenes in John's salon. It was almost destined since a lot of people who came to get serviced were entertainers. Everywhere they went was a show.

Stacey had been doing my hair for the past couple of months. She was the best stylist up in the shop. Being that she was from the east coast, she could do the California press thing as well as a roller wrap. Every black woman in L.A. either got a press or a weave. I was faithful to the perm and the roller set wrap. Sometimes I would have to get a weave when I went on tour. My hair would sweat out so easily when I danced. Stacey had moved to California with her uncle about a year before. She was always talking about how God was going to do something new out in L.A.

Stacey's uncle was known in the church in Los Angeles. He wasn't a pastor, but he spoke at different churches from time to time. He was known as Minister Earl Cooper.

I wasn't sure about the whole "Christian" thing and about Jesus being the only way to God. However, I had to admit, Stacey seemed really serious about it all.

"Stacey?" I asked, thinking intently. "Can I ask you a question?"

"Sure, what's up?" She sat me back in her chair to start rolling my hair up so I could sit under the drier.

"Are you really waiting until you're *married* to have sex?"

She looked back, smiled and said, "Everyday I strive to obey God in every area of my life. So the answer to your question is 'yes'."

"So," I continued, "Do you really think a man could wait? Until marriage?"

"If he's a man of God he could. Hey, it's not easy. Trust me. It's a day-by-day process, but I really enjoy living life in the presence of God. There's so much peace and there are days when I have joy even though everything around me is going crazy—ya know?" Stacey was smiling even harder.

"So..." I asked slowly, "How *long* has it been since, you know..."

"Since I had sex?" Stacey laughed. "Girl, two going on three years."

"Dammmmnnnnnnnn!" I said in shock. I had never heard of any one who'd had sex say that they hadn't done it in like three years...f-*that*! (I felt like, even if I cursed in my thoughts that Stacey could still hear me, so I tried not to) I didn't see how anyone who had gotten some good dick could just 'stop' having sex. I kind of wondered if Stacey was telling the truth. She might've been telling the truth, though. Like I said, she *was* a little "different".

"Girl, I only do it by the power of the Holy Spirit. God still amazes me. If you really *want* to obey and love him, he'll show you how, trust me. I remember being honest with God by saying, 'Hey, I can't do this'. God then showed me and every one else around me just how real he is by 'keeping' me and giving me the strength to do it. God loves to use those who seem like they are least likely to be used. That way, he gets the glory and all the recognition. Girl, I know God is real if he can change *me*. If me, of *all* people can abstain from having sex for going on three years, then you *know* he's real!" Stacey started laughing again. I was just trying to take everything in.

"If you ever want to go to church with me, let me know." She was still smiling. Did she ever get tired of smiling?

"Maybe one day," I said. Although I hoped she wasn't holding her breath. I couldn't see me being some Holy Roller. Most of them were fakin' anyway.

"Are you saved?" she asked.

"Yeah, I got saved and baptized when I was like eight," I laughed. Stacey didn't.

"For real, I believe in God," I said, getting serious. "I pray." I added.

"Okay," Stacey said without smiling. "You know nothing ever happens by mistake. We're definitely having this conversation for a reason. I'll be praying for ya, Miss Lady. I'm here if you need me."

"Thanks," I said with a half smile on my face.

"Aight, girl—let's get your hair hooked up." Stacey changed the subject. Then she said, "And another thing, don't be letting nobody steal your joy. You *too pretty* to be frownin'...for real. Don't be putting my work to shame. You know you my best customer. I get like ten referrals from you at a time. Don't play!"

"Stacey you crazy," I laughed. It's like Stacey knew what was goin' on between John John and I, even though I didn't tell her anything.

I'd been struggling to stay happy those days. Being John's girl wasn't everything it was cracked up to be. I loved him, but I honestly didn't know if I trusted niggas. However, John John had had my back since day one. We talked about everything. He was my best friend.

On the real, I really didn't' know if anyone else would treat me better than John.

Chapter 11:
Love & War

Trina and I were determined to tear up the malls. We always seemed to go shopping whenever she or I got off the road. We walked through the Beverly Center for what seemed like all day. The Beverly Center had every store necessary to maintain a wardrobe. We spent an hour at the MAC Store alone. I'd been wearing MAC since I was fourteen and I was faithful. No one could make me cheat on MAC.

We were both pulling off the 'I'm fly without even trying' look. I wore my Diesel jeans, white tee, Tiffany's silver jewelry, flip-flops and Christian Dior purse, and my Christian Dior sunglasses. Trina had on her black tee, Citizens of Humanity jeans, a Gucci purse that laid around her hips and her Gucci sunglasses. Then Trina had the nerve to wear her Cartier love edition charm bracelet. Oooohh, she made me sick! That bracelet was so cute! We stood in line waiting to get some coffee from Starbucks.

I pulled out my cell and tried to call John again. He was already gone when I left that morning, and he left some money on the kitchen counter for me. I hated when he would leave like that.

John still didn't answer and it was almost evening. I tried not to worry because I knew Trina would start getting all in my business.

"Calling John again, huh?" Trina said before I could even complete my thought.

"Yeah," I said, not really wanting to entertain her questions. Trina should have been a lawyer.

"I'm tellin' you, Lady — you *doin'* too much. You need to keep him guessing. It's no way in hell that you should be calling him like five or more times in a day. Fuck that!"

"I don't feel like it right now, Trina. *Aight?*" I was more annoyed than a woman with a yeast infection.

My phone rang and it was John. I picked up the phone right away.

"Sorry, babe," were the first words I heard John say. "I've been taking care of business and I didn't want you to get worried."

"You couldn't pick up the phone just to say you were okay?" I said in disbelief.

"You know how I don't want you involved in what I do. We'll talk later. I just called to tell you that I love you. See you tonight."

"Bye." I could barely get that out as he hung up the phone.

I could feel Trina's eyes and ears on me closer than the scent of my own perfume. I refused to look at her, because I knew she was going to have something negative to say about what had just happened. Trina swore she knew everything, and she really got on my nerves at times. She was always so negative, even though she called it being "real."

I continued to order my soy chai latte, (yeah, I was real 'L.A.' for drinking soy, what can I say?) To my surprise, Trina didn't say a word.

We walked in complete silence from Starbucks until we got to the parking lot. We put our bags in Trina's trunk and sat inside the Range.

We were still silent as we drove for about a mile or two. When we reached Laurel Canyon to go over the hill to the valley, Trina finally turned off the radio and looked at me. I knew she was going to say something. It was just a matter of time.

"You know that something ain't right, Lady," Trina said without asking if she could share her thoughts. I didn't say a word, so she kept on. "John is playin' you."

"Did I *ask* you for your opinion?!" I asked angrily.

"It's not my opinion, it's what I *KNOW*." Trina said this without showing any type of emotion. I snapped back with a quickness.

"How do *you* know, Trina? You saw him cheatin?"

"No. But I've had enough niggas cheat on me before and I *know* the game."

"Whatever, Trina."

I just brushed off her statements. Just because she got cheated on didn't mean she knew when every man on the face of the earth was cheating! Besides, Trina couldn't even keep her legs closed long enough for a nigga to *be* faithful. She didn't know *every* fucking thing. *She got on my nerves!*

John John was too busy in the streets getting money to be worried about some pussy. Besides, we had sex almost every other day. How much pussy could one man get?

"You must really be whipped because you're actin' real dumb right now," Trina continued.

"Fuck you, Trina," I said without even thinking.

"I'm gonna excuse what you just said because I know you trippin off that nigga's dick. He done whipped you so bad that—"

"Trina, just take me home, aight?" I was frustrated with her insistence on proving that she knew what was best for me and everyone else in the world.

"I'm gone say it again—sleep and roll. Things are better that way. Once you start getting pressed, niggas smell desperation and they start getting real tired, real quick. My man called me at least five times today and that's all I'm gonna say."

Trina was finished so she turned the music back up. Good. I was wondering when she was going to shut the fuck up. I couldn't wait to get out of that truck before I hurt her.

Chapter 12:
Just Me & You

It's funny how life can be so surprising. I was determined to dance and there I was, *doin' it!* I was booking almost every video, every awards show, and I was consistently on tour with different artists. I was dancing. I wasn't shaking my butt all across the screen looking like some five cent ho at the strip club. I had worked with the famous choreographer Shooky Simmons at least five times since we first worked together in Lord Life's video the year before. There I was on the set of Tre's new video, getting ready for wardrobe. That day was like a reunion.

Tre' was finally going to drop his album in about a month or so, and I was playing his main girl in the video. Who would have thought that corny Tre' would be considered a sex symbol by women all over the country. Tre' was dancing in most of the video, and they needed someone to complement him well in the dance scenes. Who else would they have chosen besides me?

I had to give it to Tre', his single was really hot. He was even looking kinda *aight*, even though he was still corny. He was actually kinda cool, just a little annoying at times. He just acted that way because he had gotten so watered down from being in L.A. where the women chase the men down like Olympic track stars. Those women weren't amateurs, either. They pimped niggas so hard that I felt sorry for them. The women didn't just get their bills paid, they got rich off of other niggas' money. Niggas' had to pay to play. I wasn't mad.

That day we were shooting the scene for the video on Melrose Ave. Tre' walked past me as I was standing there and said, "See — if you weren't John's girl, I would say how good you looked right now."

"Hey, Tre'" I said laughing. He was still tired. He looked nice though. He had on this belt that made his whole outfit look like a million dollars.

I continued walking away from wardrobe, and it was really a reunion when Miss Candy the makeup artist walked up in her usual extra perky, white girl voice that you would hear from characters on T.V.

"*Oh my God!!!* Lady! How *are you*?!!!" She was loud enough for the birds to hear.

"Hi, Candy," I said, almost laughing.

"You are still sooo pretty!" she continued. "Come right on over for make-up, okay, hon?"

Was I supposed to be ugly now? Dealing with her, I thought I'd need to take a Tylenol to get through the day.

Trina walked up with Lord Life coming from the trailers, and she looked right at me. Trina had on her casual Abercrombie & Fitch sweat suit with her Nikes.

"I know you not still mad from earlier this week, are you?" she asked, smiling with an attitude.

"Girl, get out my face." I smiled back at her.

She reached out and hugged me. No one was mad anymore. I could have killed Trina earlier this week when she couldn't stay out of my business and keep her mouth shut about how she felt about John John. We could never stay mad at each other too long. It was all good now, though.

"John ain't coming?" Lord Life asked.

"Later, he had something to take care of," I said without much thought. Lord Life knew what I meant. John was Tre's road manager. However, when they weren't out on the road, he usually handled all of his "business" in between.

I knew that he wasn't concerned with coming early that day to "manage" me, since he had the entire black mafia looking after me during the day's shoot. Everyone there was cool with John and the whole entourage had their eyes on me. It might not have seemed like anyone was watching, but I was being watched.

Just as I suspected, white girl Emily came switching her white ass up to the set. She was probably working production that day, but everyone knew she came to work every available penis on the set.

She walked right past me and didn't say a word. I guessed miss nasty ass was still embarrassed from that week at John's shop. I watched her walk up to some of Lord's boys. It was just a matter of time before she'd be in the trailer giving somebody some head. She was such a ho.

Trina and I looked at each other and shook our heads. We were used to the same scenes that replayed over and over again at almost every video shoot.

"Wassup, yo," I heard John's voice say behind me. I turned around and he walked up to all of us.

"What's goin' on?" Lord Life said smiling.

"Hey, babe," John said as he kissed me. I kissed him back and noticed white girl Emily staring all down my throat as we kissed.

"What the hell is her problem?" I asked him. "Why is she all in my face?" I was ready to kick the white girl's ass.

"Maybe she thinks you're cute. She might be tired of the dick and now she's a carpet muncher."

"Whatever," I said, punching John in his arm. "All I know is she better stop staring me in my face. "

"Let me holla at you for a second," Lord interrupted, talking to John. Then he turned to me. "We'll be back".

Trina and I looked at each other and shook our heads again. Those two were always having some private meeting somewhere.

Trina and I left to go to make-up. Since Trina just came to watch, she walked over with me. I knew Trina was going to have jokes after watching me tolerate Candy. The both of them were just too funny. I couldn't help but to laugh at the facial expressions that Trina made whenever she was around Candy.

While Candy did my make-up, I thought about the past year or so living in Los Angeles. You would think we were in a dream the way everything had just come together. John and I were together, Trina and Lord Life were getting married, and I was making a living being a dancer. I hadn't really talked to my parents since I moved, and I wondered how they were. I wasn't concerned enough to pick up the phone, though. Everything was going so well that I didn't want to mess it up by bringing some mess up from B-More. I really didn't need that.

Candy finished my make-up and it was almost call time. I really had to pee, so I ran back over to the trailers to look for an available bathroom. I figured Lord's trailer would be available since he and John went to go do their business. I knocked on Lord's trailer and then opened the door quickly. I really had to go.

As soon as I walked in the trailer, my heart stopped for what seemed like death. From the moment I walked into the trailer, it seemed like everything happened in slow motion.

Almost every one of my senses didn't seem to work, except for my *sight*. All I could *see* was white girl Emily on her knees with her back turned toward me. Her head was bobbing back and forth. To add to my disbelief, I *saw* John's face scrunched up tighter than the fist that I made at the thought of beating white girl Emily's head on the ground. John was biting his lip and closing his eyes while she sucked his dick.

I started having flashbacks of that same face that I had seen more times than I could count. All I could **see** was John's face when I would go down on him. I think I remembered, right there in less than 30 seconds, every moment that I had given him head. I remembered from the first time when he showed me how to do it, to the first time I turned him out and made him say my name while he called on God. This mutha fucker was going to have to call on more than God once he **saw** me standing there.

My sense of **hearing** kicked in when I **heard** him say, "Oh my God", as he was about to cum. Those words weren't sacred to me anymore.

My sense of **touch** was turned on when I **felt** warm tears streaming down my face while my body was shaking uncontrollably.

John opened his eyes and **saw** me standing there. I watched his face turn from pleasure to embarrassment in half of a second.

"Bitch, get off me!" John said as he pushed Emily down. Emily turned around and looked at me. She smiled and licked her lips. I wanted to hurt her. I couldn't think straight anymore. I turned around and ran to the closest open trailer that I could find. While I was running, I could hear the director calling ten minutes until places.

I just sat in the trailer and cried. I felt like I was having flashbacks from over a year ago when I saw my dad cheating on my mother. I felt like I was being haunted. Everything I tried to blur in my past just rose up and slapped me in my face. It hurt so bad. I thought that John was different. I thought I wasn't going to turn into a bitter woman like Trina and other women who just seemed to go numb in order to survive out here. Life was a bitch.

From that moment on, I knew that I couldn't trust any man anymore. I thought about every time that I had suspected John John was cheating on me and how I had ignored my instincts. I thought about how he acted insecure about me cheating on him when he was guilty of cheating on me all along. All this time, *he* was guilty. He was lying to me.

The more I thought about seeing John cheat on me with my own eyes, the angrier I became. I could barely stop shaking.

"Two minutes to places," someone said as they knocked on the trailer door.

I'd been through too much to let this get to me. I got up, went into the bathroom, wiped my face and looked in the mirror.

"Just me and you," I said to myself. "All I got is you."

I realized that I couldn't trust anyone anymore.

Looking up to the sky I said, *"I don't understand all of this, I really don't. Don't I deserve to be happy for once?"* I pleaded with God.

I was angry at everyone at that point. I think I was a little mad at God. Why would he let all these things happen to me?

Now was not the time for me to break down. I had to keep going. I wanted everything to go away. I walked out of the trailer and made my way over to where they were filming the scene for the video. I continued to walk, as I built up enough strength to be on my mark for the dance scene.

"Let me talk to you for a second," John said as he grabbed my arm.

"Get the fuck off me, John," I said as I pulled away and kept walking.

"Who the fuck you talking to? I said let me talk to you for a second!" John yelled in that tone that I used to think was so manly, sexy, and firm. Now his voice sounded like one of those scenes that you couldn't look at in a scary movie.

"Places!" the director called. Everyone started to make their way to their places outside so that we could shoot the video in the hot sun. The sun seemed to shine extra hard in my face as John looked at me. I really wished that the sun could have just blinded me for a moment. I couldn't and I didn't even want to look at him. He grabbed my chin and turned it until we looked at each other face-to-face.

"Look, Lady. I messed up. I haven't lied to you, and I'm not going to lie to you now. Aight…you caught me. I didn't mean to mess up wit' that bitch. I don't even want her. I was using my phone in Lord's trailer and she came in and unbuttoned my pants. What the fuck was I supposed to do, Lady? I'm a *MAN*."

He could see I wasn't budging.

"Oh, so the one time I mess up you gonna walk out on me, huh? All this shit I do for you? *For us*?!"

I looked at him. John sounded like he was going to break up with *me*, even though *he* was the one cheating.

"Yeah. If you weren't so busy trying to be a God damned superstar and started taking care of yo' man, then maybe I wouldn't have cheated on you. Fuck this, go head and do your lil' scene. I do everything for you and you gonna hold this against me? Go head. We'll talk later when you finish your scene, superstar."

"Places!" the director repeated.

Everyone was looking at John and I. The director really called "places" again, because I was the only one that wasn't in my place yet. Everyone knew something was going on, but they couldn't hear what we were saying.

I looked at John and he had this look of arrogance on his face. He nodded his head in a way to let me know that he knew that I was going to choose dancing over him at that moment.

I turned away from John and a tear trickled down my face. I wiped it away so that no one would notice my pain. I walked over next to Tre' and waited for the music to drop.

"Oh my God, wait one second!" Candy the make up artist yelled as she flew her oreo cookie butt over to me to touch up my face. She got on my God damned nerves. I looked at her to let her know to hurry up, because I was not in the mood for her "One Black Blonde Woman Show."

I knew that once the music started and I began dancing, everything would go away.

For a brief moment, I could be free.

Chapter 14:
Hooked

I drove in silence. No radio. No cell phone. All I could hear was the sound of my turn signal as I switched lanes on the 101 Freeway.

The wind hit my face so hard that even if I tried to cry, the tears would dry up before they had a chance to reach my cheek. I was doing about 90 miles per hour.

The night seemed darker than usual, even though all of the stars shone brighter than I'd ever noticed before. I got tired of my head being flooded with thoughts, so I turned on the radio to help calm me down. Wrong move.

It seemed like every station I turned to happened to be playing a love song. I stop switching stations when I heard Sade playing. "Cherish the Day" was my song and it seemed to go perfectly with the way I coasted on the freeway. I began to think about how my daddy used to play Sade when we would ride around in his Camaro when I was little. He would strap me in the front seat and I would just lean back in my chair to let the wind hit me in my face.

For a moment, I felt like I was that little girl again. I was naïve to what the world looked like because in my world, everything was perfect. The older I became, the more I realized that shit just wasn't what it was cracked up to be. Life was like a crack-head in B-more tryin' to get another hit wit' no money—CRAZY.

I eventually reached Calabasas and made my way toward Tre's house. After what happened between John and I, I really didn't want to go home. Lord Life and Trina went over to Tre's house after the video shoot. I figured that I might as well hang out with them so I wouldn't keep thinking about what had happened earlier that day.

I pulled up to Tre's town house and parked my car. I rang the doorbell. Trina answered the door and looked at me with an unspoken sympathy that seemed to dance all over her face.

"C'mon on in, girl," she said pulling me in the door.

Tre's house was really nice. It was my first time over because John, (stupid ass), would always have a fit at the thought of me being there. Tre' had a really modern town house with all new amenities. It was a real bachelor pad. His entire apartment was decorated with a modern theme. He had a bangin' black leather sofa and every room had a flat screen TV, including the bathrooms. Trina held my hand and pulled me into Tre's bedroom so we could talk.

Tre's bedroom walls were a nice tan color and his bed looked like something out of a hotel. His comforter was a strong, manly dark blue, and he had tan pillows to accent. We sat on his chocolate brown leather chaise.

"You okay?" Trina asked in a concerned, almost motherly voice.

"Yeah, I'm aight," I said calmly.

"What you gonna do?"

"Honestly, Trina, I don't even know. John is so involved in my life *and* my career."

I could see in Trina's eyes that she'd been where I was before. I didn't have to say much for her to understand what was going on in my heart.

"Well," she said, "You can always stay with Lord and I if you need to, you know that." Trina paused for a moment. "I know you still love him. The shit ain't fair. Just because you want to stop loving somebody doesn't mean that your heart listens to what you tell it to do. Sometimes I just want to take my heart out and kick its ass if it had one."

We both laughed.

"You can't give a man your everything, girl. When it's over, you won't have nothing left. Nothing to live for — "

"I don't feel like talking about it anymore," I cut Trina off.

"I understand," she said, without hesitation.

We both got up and went into the living room where Lord Life and Tre' were sitting around talking and drinking. They were sitting there having a debate about music, as usual.

Being on tour with different artists, I often wondered if musicians had anything else to talk about but music. I learned real quickly that musicians were an interesting species. A lot of musicians that I hung out with on tour were hos. A lot of them didn't have respect for women. There were a select few who were cool though. Some of the most unknown musicians had the biggest egos. It was like their heads blew up once they played for a major star on tour, and they just knew they were the shit.

They had groupies, too. If a major artist had groupies, then you'd best believe that every musician on tour with him had groupies as well. I really thought it was like an unsaid rule: musician = arrogant + flaky + ho/groupies (musician equaled arrogant plus flaky plus ho, divided by groupies). Most musicians had one of the personalities in the equation. All they did was talk about how nice so and so was on the keys, how talented so and so was on the bass, and how so and so did his thing at a set last night. Who cared?

I did meet a select few who were honest family men, though. I really appreciated my musician friends who kept it real and were loyal to their women. The other ones—I kept at arm's length. Some musicians had such an infamous rep that if you even hung out wit' em', everyone would think y'all were fuckin'. I didn't need that drama.

Oh, and don't let someone come around the circle and not be "known." They weren't going to have any conversation for them. Trust and believe, if you had placements, (songs that you wrote that played on the radio), they already knew it before you could even offer the information. If you didn't have any placements, they knew you weren't worth the conversation. It was the nature of the game.

They would come off tour after having enough sex for at least two men, and play for the church. I would think to myself, "Don't the pastors know what they be doin?" I thought it was kind of weird. I guess God knew their hearts when they did 'who knows what' on tour and came back to church like nothing happened. There was a lot of contradiction, if you asked me. But then who was I to say? I didn't even go to church every Sunday, and that's probably why I didn't.

Trina interrupted Tre' and Lord by throwing a pack of cards on the coffee table in front of them.

"Spades, nigga—what?" Trina challenged. "Me and my girl against you sorry ass losers."

"I don't wanna hurt your feelings, babe," Lord Life laughed.

"Bring it!" Trina said again.

"Hold up," Tre' said, looking at Trina and I. "You two be cheatin'. Lady and I gonna be partners."

"Okaaayyy..." Trina said, smiling and looking at me with a look that told me that Tre' was trying to pursue me.

I had never given Tre' a millisecond of my time. I had always brushed him off from day one and he'd kept pursuing me. He always respected John, so he never really pushed up too hard. He'd probably gotten word that John got busted. Trina couldn't keep her mouth shut to save her life.

As Trina dealt the first hand, I could see Tre' looking at me right in my face. I wouldn't look at him, but I could feel him *on* me. When I looked up at him, he had this sort of innocent stare. It was the stare that John gave me when he would look at me from across the room. It was as if he was just admiring us being together or something. Tre' had that same stare. I made a face that asked him, "What the hell are you staring at me for" and smiled. Tre' smiled back.

I was beginning to think that Trina was right when she would tell me that men liked bitches. It seemed like they loved it when you treated them like trash, and walked all over them like concrete pavement. When you were nice and concerned, they abused you. As soon as you started giving a damn about a nigga, he would turn on you faster than you would turn the cold water on after burning your finger with the hot water in the sink.

Tre' just kept staring at me, and I started to feel what he was thinking. That nigga was horny. I wished he would just say it instead of staring me in my face. He was trying to act like he was genuinely interested in me. John John and I were probably going to break up, and I hadn't really "had some" since before the tour I'd finished the week before. That was a little over two months. I looked at Tre' and smiled back. He was too persistent. I'd heard he would make women crazy! I couldn't see why because he was so corny. I'd heard stories about girls checking his voicemail, slashing his tires, and flipping through his windows trying to catch him screwin' some other chick. He knew he wasn't innocent. Wasn't no nigga gonna have me acting like some crazed chick. *He really had women flipping through windows...*

His eyes lit up when I licked the dryness from my lips. Damn, this nigga was thirsty. He was acting like a lil' fiend over there. I took a good look at him and noticed how his lips made "the famous rapper that we all know who has the best lips" be put to shame.

We were on our last hand and the pressure was on. It was one intense game of spades. Trina and Lord might as well have given up at that moment. Tre' just kept pulling out spades until we had ten books in one hand. Game over.

We jumped up and Tre' pulled me close to give me a celebration hug. His strong arms made my body cave in from my waist down. Nobody had ever had that effect on me before.

"Aight, I'm out," Lord Life barely said, with sleepiness in his voice. " See y'all tomorrow."

Tre' interrupted. "You can stay here if you'd like, Lady. I have an extra room."

Trina looked at me as her face said, "Oooohhhh...girl." She waited for me to reply. At that moment I could hear her words, "You better learn how to sleep and roll ..." It's amazing how you never forget certain words that people say to you. At that moment, hearing those words lit' something deep down inside of me that I never even knew existed. There I was having the thought of sexin' Tre. The funny part is, I used to always get on Trina for being a ho. She would hide it from everyone out in Hollywood because she was so selective with who she slept with. She'd only messed with Chris Harris (the NBA Player) and Lord Life. When she needed some dick, she would screw some random nigga or one of her "friends" back in B-more when she went to visit. I knew the truth.

"You don't mind if I stay in your guest room?" I responded with hardly any hesitation.

"Naw," Tre' said, faster than a man who was cumming after having two minutes of sex.

"Aight, girl—call me if you need me," Trina said. Then she whispered, "Don't do nothing I wouldn't do." She and Lord got up to walk toward the front door.

I watched them both walk out the door to take that *long* drive to Wilshire Boulevard so they could get back to their condo. I felt sorry for them. Knowing Lord Life, they would get there in less than twenty-five minutes. He drove like he still lived in New York. It should have been about a forty-minute drive.

I looked at Tre' as he locked the front door, and he looked at me not knowing what to do. I think he was in shock that I was staying the night.

"Here, let me show you to the guest room." He led me down the halls.

We walked until we reached a room that was all cream with sepia pictures all over the walls. The bed was all white with a white canopy that draped over it. It was so weird. It kind of reminded me of being back in my house in B-more, sleeping under my canopy.

"I'll be over in the next room, call me if you need to," Tre' offered politely. "Help yourself to anything in the house."

"Can I hold some boxer shorts and a t-shirt?' I asked without much thought.

Tre' went into his room and came back with a Polo t-shirt and some boxer shorts. He looked at me to make sure that I didn't need anything else, and then he left the room. It didn't really hit me that I was spending the night at Tre' house until I started to get undressed. John John's house had been the only house I'd stayed over at, and we lived together. It kinda felt a little weird, but *everything* had been weird that entire day, if you asked me.

I got under the covers but I couldn't sleep. It was the first time that I had even attempted to rest all day. I had almost blocked out what happened between John and I. I was tired of crying. Thinking about it got old real quick. It seemed like I had been living some fantasy life before I saw John cheating on me.

I almost thought that losing my virginity so late was a bad thing. Where would I go from there? Most women lost their virginity at like fourteen, and they would cry and talk about how their boyfriend had played them and how they were hurt. Now, there I was thinking the same thing, but I was a grown ass woman. I didn't even know how to date. I mean, most women I knew had "friends", (sex partners). No one really "dated" anymore. All of the women that I knew seemed kinda bitter. They would meet a guy, he would take them out for a couple of weeks and then they would sleep together. Shit, most of them didn't even wait three days, let alone a day.

I thought about my hair stylist, Stacey, and how she was waiting until she was married to have sex. She was the only person that I knew who even said that. To be honest, I started to think that she was the only person in America who would have enough nerve to *say* it, let alone *do* it.

That made me wonder, *"What man in America would actually marry her?"* Most men couldn't even be faithful to the women who were giving up the ass every night. What man would even last longer than a week, (maybe two, if you were lucky) with NO SEX? I wondered if she was just going around saying it because it sounded good and if she was secretly having sex. It was one thing to be a virgin; it was another thing to be a grown ass woman with needs.

There I was, thinking so hard that I couldn't even sleep. I got up out of my bed and walked over to Tre's room. I could see his TV flickering in the hall. When I walked in, he was watching the Christian Channel. He noticed me standing in the doorway, and he sat up. He was still up too.

"You aight?" he asked, seeming concerned.

"I can't sleep," I said, still standing in the doorway.

"I usually watch the Christian channel when I can't sleep," Tre' said, offering an explanation.

"Is that right..." I said, with a tiny smile on my face.

"What?" he asked. "I *grew* up in the church. I believe in God. "

"Why you not singing Gospel?" I asked sarcastically.

"Why don't you quit dancing in the videos and on tours and be a Praise Dancer?" He had a quick comeback.

I laughed when I thought to myself that I would be dead ass broke if I did that. I couldn't say a word.

"Yeah, thought so." Tre laughed too. "Naw, all jokes aside. I wanted to do Gospel, but you can't get money doin' that. Most people don't go mainstream. My grandma raised me when my mom and dad left, and I remember seeing her struggle just to keep the lights on. I made a promise to myself that I wouldn't see her struggle like that for the rest of my life. "

I got tired of standing in the doorway, so I made my way to the edge of Tre's bed. I sat down without any thought. He kept talking.

"I would work my ass of in the studio, because I knew that I had to 'come up' so that my family could 'come up'. I refused to be some broke ass, no life nigga like my father." He wore a look of hurt. "Lord Life and I been best friends since we were in middle school. He used to come to church wit' me from time to time, but he wasn't really into it like that. He wasn't feeling the whole church thing because he had to go home to a father that whipped his ass. He felt like Jesus wasn't saving him from that. He watched his father beat the shit out of his mother until his mom got locked up for stabbing his dad in self defense when he was fourteen."

"Damn," I said. I couldn't really say much to that.

"Yeah...when his mom got locked up he had to take care of himself. Then you knew what time it was."

Tre' looked at me as he said this, because he knew that I knew. Lord always talked about being on his own, hustlin' and being a gangsta in his songs.

Tre' continued. "Most people wonder if he really lived that life he talks about in his songs because it seems so real when he talks about it. Man, that shit *was* real. I was right there."

Tre' noticed how involved I was while he was telling me the story.

"I don't know why I am telling you all of this," Tre' said calmly, in disbelief.

"It's all good," I said. "I know how it is. You ain't telling me nothing I ain't ever heard, seen, or experienced growing up in B-more."

"Yeah, B-more is mad ghetto," Tre' laughed.

"Uh huh, like you ain't!" I responded, rolling my eyes.

I noticed that Tre' and I could just talk easily. We were talking like we'd grown up together. He continued to tell me how he would go to church every Sunday until he was like sixteen, and how he stopped going when he noticed that a lot of folks were living double lives. He told me about how he got his first piece of ass when he was fourteen from this lil' girl in Sunday school. I told him how I left when I was about twelve when I saw some of the same stuff he was telling me. We both agreed that we didn't think that you had to go to church every Sunday in order to get into heaven.

"Yeah, so that's why I'm not doing Gospel," Tre' said. "God and I talk. I thank him for being able to sing. I know it's a gift. I try to live right. I just ask for forgiveness every day. God knows my heart."

I looked at Tre' in a way that I'd never looked at him before. He was kinda cool. It was cute the way his dimples would show when he would grin a little. I could almost see the little boy deep down underneath all of that sex symbol and thug image. I smiled.

"What's the smile for, Miss Lady?" Tre' asked. "What you over there thinking?' He got all up in my face.

"Nothing, boy." I pushed his face away. It seemed like the more we talked the closer we got, mentally and physically. The more we talked the more I moved closer to Tre' on his bed. Before I realized it, we were sitting right next to each other.

"Mind yo' business," I laughed.

"Shit, you might be over there trying to set a nigga up!" Tre' said in a joking manner. "All this information I done told you."

"You the one I need to be worried about. You done seduced me by talking my damn ear off and got me sittin next to you in *yo'* bed." I said peeping game.

"Damn, you noticed?" Tre' asked.

"Shut up, yo!" I laughed as I hit him on the arm.

Tre' leaned over and kissed me. I kissed him back. It was natural.

At that moment I understood how a woman could get caught up in the moment. When he kissed me, I didn't think of anything else but the moment. Right there, as I kissed Tre' in his bed, I became a part of the majority of women who "didn't mean to do it".

I still loved John, even though I was in the bed with Tre'. Right then, not only was I horny, but I needed what Tre' was giving me at that very moment: attention, affection, and the feeling that things were exactly the way that they should be. I really wanted to break up with John but I didn't know if I could. My heart still wanted to be with him, even though it hurt me at the very thought of even kissing him again. Even though I wanted to end the relationship with John, I couldn't break free yet. I was **hooked**.

I guess you get used to a person after a while. I used to think that women who would stay with lyin', crazy, cheatin' men, (like my mother for instance), were stupid. Now, I was stupid.

One thing's for sure, I didn't belong to John *that* night. There was no way that I, the "Queen", could belong to John when I was lettin' Tre' meet the "Princess" between my legs.

That night, I cheated on John Anderson.

Chapter 15:
Game of Chess

I was driving home to face the hard truth: I had been unfaithful. And there was another problem — Tre' was better in bed than John John. He had fucked the shit out of me. Now I saw why Tre' had women flipping through windows. I was ready to do cartwheels just thinking about that night. Or should I say, that morning. I screamed so loud that I'm surprised nobody called the cops.

It was off the hook but I felt bad. I didn't know what Tre' would think of me. He probably thought I was some ho. He probably looked at me totally different from before. My worst nightmare had become a reality. I'd had sex with someone and we weren't even in a relationship. Shit, I was in a relationship and had sex with someone who I wasn't in a relationship with. I cheated. I'd messed up twice in one night.

It was a wonderful thing, though. Tre' got up and cooked me breakfast that morning. Then we took a shower together and did it again.

By twelve in the afternoon my cell phone had thirty-five missed calls on it. They were all John. I definitely wasn't gonna go home. I called Trina and let her know that I was on my way to her place. I turned off the Wilshire exit off of the 405 Freeway. I figured that I would go to Lord and Trina's house until I could get my head straight.

I got stuck in traffic for a minute as I drove less than a quarter of a mile away from the freeway. Lord and Trina lived in a really nice condo close to USC's campus. I pulled up to the front of the building and a guy from the valet service came over to park my truck. Every time I visited their home it was like visiting a high-class hotel.

I got off the elevator and knocked on Trina and Lord's door. Trina answered the door, ready to gossip.

"Girl, John John called me like ten times looking for you," she said. "I told him I didn't know where you were. Shit, it was none of his God-damned business."

"Thanks," I said, as I followed her to the kitchen.

The entire condo had marble floors with the exception of the carpet in the bedrooms. It sort of had the same look Trina had in her old apartment in the valley. It was definitely modern traditional. The only difference now was that this girl had the budget of a rich bitch. There were beautiful chandeliers hanging in the entrance as well as the dining room. Everything in the living room and dining room was cream. It was a matter of time before NTV Cribs would be over to do a show. Lord had a house in Florida that would just make you pee on yourself as soon as you walked in it; it ain't make no sense how phat that house was. The first time I walked up in there, I started sweatin'.

"Have you ever cheated on your man before?" I asked, as I lifted myself up to sit on the counter top.

"Oooohhh, you *did* it to Tre'," Trina said knowingly. "I *knew* it."

"What?" I said, like it wasn't obvious.

"C'mon now, that nigga been tryin to smell, let alone *touch* your coochie for like over a year!" We laughed as Trina continued. " Last night I saw him looking like one of those dirty boys in third grade, the ones that always seemed to catch us when we used to play seven eleven at school."

We both yelled and laughed at the same time. "Seven pumps, eleven kisses!"

I had advanced way past the third grade with the lil' episode I had just pulled. I didn't know what I was going to do next. I guessed I had to face John eventually. The reality was that he paid most of the bills; I couldn't afford to just up and leave.

Everything was so "off." Tre' and I had slept together and he hadn't called me since I left his house. I knew it had only been an hour or so, but he could have at least called. I started to feel like I was expecting him to be my man or something. It just seemed weird to sleep with him and then act like nothing ever happened. On another note, I wasn't trying to be in no relationship no time soon. I didn't trust niggas.

I felt like before everything changed with John John, I had been skipping through the tulips, looking like some dumb ass. That day I realized that the hope I used to have was dead. Niggas wasn't shit.

"Bitch, why you keep looking at your phone?" Trina pried as usual. "Dang, I heard Tre' be having girls looking retarded. You over there staring at your phone, 'bout to drool."

"Shut up!" I said, laughing at Trina's crazy butt. "Girl, I'm pressed like a muthafucker over here. I ain't *even gonna lie to you*."

"I see," Trina said, laughing. "He got you over there looking all whipped and shit!"

I *was* a little overly excited. No one had ever made me scream to the top of my lungs before, not even John. I was ready to go back over to Tre's house. I couldn't get my mind right.

Ring.

My phone rang and as I reached to grab it, Trina interrupted.

"Who is it?" she asked.

"Tre'," I said, going for my phone faster than a runner going for a gold medal in the Olympics.

"Answer the phone, talk for like one minute, and then tell him you'll call him back without giving him a reason. Don't tell him you're over here talking to me either." Her eyes were insistent. "*Just do what I say…*"

"Hello," I answered. "Working on something…. I can't tell you that. Is that right…"

Trina looked at me and nodded to let me know to hang up the phone. We looked like we were playing a serious game of charades.

"Naw, I haven't even talked to Trina. Look, let me call you right back." I hung up the phone before Tre' could say goodbye.

"That's what I'm talking 'bout," Trina said. "Never EVER let him hang up first. I'm telling you, *girl* — if you play your cards right, you could have that good ass dick fo' life!"

We laughed. As soon as Trina finished what she had to say, Tre' called my phone right back. I didn't pick it up because Trina had explained that men like the chase. Tre' was used to women acting all crazy after he'd had sex with them. Being that I wasn't acting pressed, (even though I actually was), he didn't know what to do. Trina insisted that you had to *train* a nigga to act right.

"**Life is like a game of chess** — you gotta always know what the nigga's next move is before you make yours," Trina said, real cocky. "See, most women don't know how to play chess. But the ones who do, kick ass. You gotta play to win."

I was starting to see the world for what it really was. Crazy as hell.

Chapter 16: Who's Your Daddy Now?

I turned the knob to the door of my house slowly, anticipating what would jump off when I walked through the door. I had stayed at Trina's all day, and it was now eleven o'clock at night. I hadn't been home for going on two days. John and I still lived in our apartment in the valley, and I knew he was home because I saw his BMW in the parking lot.

I walked through the door and saw him sitting on the sofa. He looked at me as the TV watched him. No one said a word for a good five minutes. Then...

"Where the fuck you been?" John asked firmly. "You couldn't pick up your fucking phone?"

"I'm sorry," I surprisingly said, as warm tears streamed down my face. All those thoughts about me being "hard" had stopped right outside the door. Coming back into the apartment took me to an emotional place that I couldn't compete with. I couldn't believe how one day could fuck up a whole year of happiness. I tried to explain myself.

"I couldn't look at you John," I said, breaking down. "You hurt me. That's why I couldn't come home."

I was experiencing the powerful effects of being powerless. I felt so weak. It was like he had a hold over me that I couldn't break free from. It was like a sick magnetic effect that locked me in if I got close enough. And I was close. I felt sick to my stomach from thinking too hard.

"So you decided to 'get even' by not coming home?" John questioned. "I see you don't give a fuck about US! I'm sitting here, trying to work shit out, AND YOU OUT IN THE MUTHA FUCKIN' STREETS!" John yelled loud enough for the entire building to hear.

"Fuck you!" I screamed back with tears in my eyes. "You were my first and only, and you had the nerve to fucking cheat on me with dirty ass Emily!"

I realized that I'd just told a lie—John wasn't my "only" anymore. But what he didn't know wouldn't hurt him. Since I cheated on him with Tre', we were even.

We argued for at least an hour. I'd never seen John lose his cool like that. We battled so hard that I thought that he was going to hit me at one point. He said some ugly things and I said some ugly things back. The whole thing was just ugly.

My face was wet with tears and John looked like he wanted to punch the wall out. Eventually, he was the only person arguing. I didn't have much to say. I was in shock. My silence made him even angrier.

"Fuck you!" John yelled. "I knew you weren't wife material no way. We ain't even married, and you ready to walk out on a nigga? Silly ass ho."

I felt worthless. I couldn't say anything in response to what he'd just said to me. I thought that John would be my one and only. I thought we would be married soon. Now I realized that he wasn't planning on being with me forever. I saw the hard but real truth: the only real commitment was marriage. I could hear my mom's voice as I remembered what she used to always tell me:

> *"Never fall completely in love, never give him your heart, never tell him everything, (especially how many sex partners you've had), never check his voicemail, never give it up before three months, (if you do, wait at least three more months to make up for the slip up), and never say never. Oh, and one more important thing--the only real commitment is marriage. Boyfriends always cheat."*

Of all people, John knew what had happened with my dad. I thought he wouldn't hurt me, not like that. I thought I would always feel safe. I almost thought he would be perfect. I thought we were the perfect couple. I was wrong.

I grabbed my purse and my keys to leave. I couldn't take it anymore. As far as I was concerned—it was over between us. John saw me trying to leave and grabbed my arm.

"Lady, stay," he said effortlessly, as he calmed down a little.

"Let go so I can leave, John."

John grabbed me harder, and his grip insisted that he wasn't going to let me leave. He grabbed my purse and threw it on the floor. "Aw hell naw," I thought to myself. "This Negro is trippin'!"

"I said stay," he said forcefully. That was the end of him being calm.

I put my keys down and he let me go. He didn't say a word. I decided that I would escape at that moment by going to bed. Maybe when I woke up it would all be *over*. I walked into our bedroom and shut the door. Sleep. Peace. That's all I wanted.

■■■

I felt John climb on top of me while I was half asleep, as the light from the morning sun made its way through our bedroom blinds. The room had a certain quiet nature about it. Normally around this time, John would make it a point to wake me up by making love to me. It was something that was part of the routine of things. That morning, I wanted to be left alone. He *had* just called me a "silly ho" and other names the night before. I was determined that I was going to end the relationship and leave as soon as things calmed down. I couldn't take it anymore.

That night, my worries had turned to nightmares and I really didn't have much success with sleep. That morning, the promise of a new day and the possibility of waking up to everything just being a dream was shattered when I realized I was unofficially in hell.

John was adjusting his boxers so that he could get himself inside of me with ease. I didn't want him inside of me that morning. I didn't even want to *be* with him anymore. He had made me feel like I was some long-term piece of ass that he just might decide to keep or get rid of whenever he felt like it. My body was dead. My emotions were shut off and I refused to feel. As I could feel John trying harder than usual to get himself inside of me, I tried to move away. He grabbed me and held me down to finish what he'd started.

"John...no..." I muttered softly. "No!" I said it loud enough for him to hear.

"Don't try to close your legs now," John said without raising his voice. "It's too late for all that."

Those words pierced me so hard that I shut down. I wouldn't look at him as he kept holding me down. I couldn't even find enough strength to fight back. I just laid there, unable to move.

" Oh, so you gonna run the fucking streets *and then not give it to Daddy*?" John continued.

John pushed his way inside of me as I laid as still as a dead person. He stroked inside of me as if he thought he was making love to me. He didn't notice or didn't care that I wasn't giving myself back to him. The more his sperm built up in his penis waiting to break free, the more forceful he got with pushing himself inside of me.

"Who's...your...daddy," John said in rhythm with every pump. He was waiting for me to answer so that he could put an end to it all.

I looked him in his eyes and saw nothing but darkness. He looked back at me, demanding the answer he'd always gotten. I was empty. Every tear of mine had already run away from me the night before. After they'd left me, I was left with nothing but a bad taste in my mouth. I guessed that's how women got bitter. What else could you be when your "sweet thang" turned sour. The longer I took to answer, the more he pumped harder.

I looked him in the eyes. I couldn't believe that it was him. I felt like I was looking the devil in the face. If the devil was using someone that morning, it had to be John. Sometimes the devil can feel so close that you feel like he's breathing down your neck. It was as if he was stalking me and refused to let me go. I wanted it to be over. I had no choice but to agree with him.

"You are," I barely said, pushing the words out of my mouth loud enough for him to hear.

He nutted at that very moment. As he laid on me, I felt like I was stuck at the bottom of the sea and the water refused to let me rise to the top. I was surprised that I was still breathing.

"Damn," he said softly, in relief. He was satisfied. I didn't have anything left.

John got up and went into the bathroom to clean up. After he finished, he walked into the other room and left me in the bedroom.

I just stared at the wall. If anyone had asked me what I was thinking about at that moment, I would've said 'nothing.' If anyone had asked me what had just happened, I would've said 'nothing.' I was in denial.

Something happens to you when a person takes yo' shit. Especially when they take something from you that's not as easy as your money or your purse. Especially when the thief is someone who you've given it to before, but he decides to take more than what you can give. Something happens when you tell him "no" and he decides "yes", because it's not even yours to say anymore. According to John, it was his. Maybe John thought that he had paid for it by then, since he basically took care of me. I hadn't thought I was for sale. I guess I was...

It takes a while for your brain to catch up with your body when you've been raped. It's as if your brain doesn't expect for your body to do something that your brain didn't tell it to do. My brain didn't tell me to sleep with John, but my body slept with John anyway. John might as well have slept with a dead person. I started to feel like everything was my fault because I had been so stupid. I should have just ended it when I saw him cheatin'.

"Lady, you want some breakfast?" John peeked his head into the bedroom, holding a loaf of bread.

"I'm good," I replied, without looking at him. I was convinced that the nigga was crazy. I wanted out.

I got up and took a shower. I felt like some dirty, nasty ho. Even after the shower, I still felt dirty. I guessed it would all go away eventually, just like everything else. In the meantime I just stared at the wall, not saying a word. Maybe I could make some sense of it all.

When it came to sex from that moment on, I was emotionally retarded. I was convinced that most people were too. How else could anyone survive in this world with normal emotions?

Chapter 17:
Life Goes On

Water has always been so soothing to me. Even the sound of it makes me relax, even in the craziest of times. It has the ability to change everything around it, especially when it rains.

I sat in the chair with my head in the bowl as the water danced in my hair. Stacey massaged my head while she washed my hair. Stacey had a way of washing hair that would make you feel as though she was washing every problem out with the dirt. I drifted off to sleep while the water hit my scalp like a waterfall on a get away island. Getting my hair done was my vacation.

It had been a week since John and I had broken up, gotten back together, broken up again, and gotten back together again. I stayed with him, or should I say, he stayed with me. It was sick the way he was able to control me. Every time I even thought about breaking free, I couldn't follow through with it. I was stuck. The real sick thing about it was the fact that we still made love like nothing ever happened. It was amazing how a woman could forgive. It was also amazing how a woman could be so dead, but her emotions could still be alive. We made love but it was never quite the same. We just did it so we could seem normal.

We were still together, even though we had both cheated. John John never found out my secret. As far as he was concerned, I had stayed at Trina's house that night. I found out really quick that men were dumb when it came to a woman cheating. Maybe his ego had stepped in the way and blocked his vision. He never could fully figure out if I really did anything that night. I knew what happened but I wasn't going to tell him.

Ring.

"Wassup," I said as I picked up my cell. I felt John looking at me from across the room. He was all *in* my grill. I couldn't even pee without him watching me. That was nothing new. His guilty ass...

"Yeah...aight...." I continued on the phone as Stacey combed out my hair. It was Tre' on the other end of the line.

"I'm a see you on Sunday, right?" he asked.

"*I said aigh*t," I answered again. I had already told that pressed Negro that I would go. It was only Tuesday and he was calling me about Sunday.

"Aight, ma" Tre' said. "Meet me at Trina's around seven. Later."

I hung up the phone and John probably thought I was talking to Trina because I showed no emotion. John took his eyes off of me once he saw that I wasn't on the phone anymore. He continued talking to one of the barbers.

The salon was packed as usual. The men on the other side were talking about sports and their other usual topics of discussion. Every time they saw a fine woman walk past, they would all stop talking and just look. Then they would look at each other with faces that said, *"Damnnnnn."*

I hadn't seen white girl Emily around the shop after the incident. I was pretty sure that I would see her on another video set. I hoped I wouldn't, because I would beat her ass on sight.

"So, you want the usual, boo?" Stacey asked.

" Uh-huh," I said nonchalantly. "Can I ask you a question?"

"Okay," Stacey said, concerned. "What's going on?"

Stacey was always so attentive. It was as if she really cared. She was really easy to talk to. She never asked me about my personal business, and I noticed she never talked too much about hers. That was weird for two females who talked almost every week. She also never really talked about the latest gossip in the shop, even though I knew that she knew "the business." People always seemed to go to her for advice. I would notice that women would sit in her chair and just *talk*. Stacey never seemed to mind, either.

"So," I continued, "why you waiting until you get married to have sex again? You really don't be doin' nothing? You know you got some toys!"

I looked at Stacey, trying to see her reaction. She wasn't even moved by my comment.

I didn't understand how she could be so damn calm all the time.

"You can't serve two masters," she said. "I'm waiting because I love God." She spoke without hesitation.

"So just cause you waitin' until you married means that you love God? What about people who claim they love God and they steal or lie on their taxes." I was being sarcastic on purpose. I wanted to know what Stacey was gonna have to say to *that*.

Stacey responded with patience. "To love God is to obey God. That which you yield your members to, meaning your body or your thoughts, becomes your master. No one can serve two masters. You either love one or hate the other."

"So just because you sleep with someone that means that the person becomes your master?" I asked sarcastically. I *had* to hear this…

"If you're having sex before marriage, are you obeying God?" Stacey asked.

Stacey had a point.

"So how do you figure sex before marriage is a sin?" I asked, wanting to really know the truth.

"Here." She threw a Bible on my lap. "Go to Ephesians 5:3 and read what it says."

I looked in the table of contents and started looking for the page number. Stacey saw me looking for the chapter and turned directly to the scripture for me. It read:

"But among you there must not be even a hint of sexual immorality,

or of any kind of impurity, or of greed, because these are improper for God's people."

"Keep reading", Stacey said.

"Nor should there be obscenity, foolish talk or coarse joking, which are out of place, but rather thanksgiving. For of this you can be sure: No immoral, impure or greedy person—such a man is an idolater—has any inheritance in the kingdom Christ and of God..."

"Alright stop," Stacey said, turning the pages. "Read Galatians 5:19 to 21."

It read:

"The acts of the sinful nature are obvious: sexual immorality, impurity and debauchery; idolatry and witchcraft; fits of rage, selfish ambition, dissensions, factions and envy; drunkenness, orgies, and the like. I warn you, as I did before, that those who live like this will not inherit the kingdom of God."

"So the whole world must be going to hell then," was the first thing that came out of my mouth. At one time I'd seen at least five examples of what she'd just mentioned *all up* in the church. Plus, I still hadn't read anything about "no sex before marriage" specifically. Sexual immorality could mean anything. Back in that day was different from modern times. And today, most people were fuckin'. Plus, men wrote the Bible. They could have slipped anything in there while no one was looking. Plus, I asked for forgiveness every night when I prayed to God.

"You're not supposed to just go around *tryin'* to sin because you think God will forgive you or that he knows your heart," Stacey continued. "Yes, he knows your heart, and he also knows those who really want to live for him. He'll enable you to live for him if you really want to."

Stacey didn't say anything else for a moment. She was quiet. She wasn't as easy to read as usual. I broke the silence.

"I'm not feeling the whole going to church all the time, either," I stated firmly. "Just because you go to church all the time doesn't mean you gonna make it into heaven. I've seen almost everything you just mentioned in the Bible up in the church."

"You'll know when someone is living for God," Stacey replied. "Sometimes they don't have to say a word. You'll see it in their actions and how they treat people. No good tree bears bad fruit."

"Hmm," I thought to myself, "can't nobody be perfect." Plus, there were a whole bunch of bad apples up in the church.

"Everyone comes up in church with 'something' they're dealing with," Stacey continued. "Now it's a problem when people who go to church or even say that they are 'saved' are not even trying to get right before the Lord. It's an ongoing process for me. If I wake up and declare that I am perfect, without any flaws, and I ain't chillin' up in heaven sippin' lemonade wit' Jesus, then you *know* there's a problem. That doesn't stop me from striving for perfection, meaning putting up some real effort to please God everyday I wake up."

Stacey kept talking at she starting setting my hair. "When God delivers you from things, you want to serve more, give more. A lot of times when I go to church, I look to give and not to get. Somebody may need prayer or a kind word. Plus, my pastor can *preaacch*. Church is good *all* the time. I need the Word. I never thought I would be going to church like this. I realized that I couldn't live this life by myself. That's why being filled with the Holy Spirit is important. I go to church, because I need God more than ever in my life. I'm up in there all day Sunday, Wednesday, and sometimes other times during the week. I look forward to going to church. I have my moments when I don't feel like going, *keep it real*, but when I get there it's all good."

Stacey was smiling all hard, as usual. Was she for real? Who *wanted* to go to church that much? *Shoot*, I could barely get my butt up in there on Sunday mornings let alone every day of the week. All day Sunday, even in the evenings? Why was she going all day? Three hours a week was enough! Stacey's face was glowing. She got really excited when she talked about the Lord. Don't get me wrong, I enjoyed the Lord, but people just be taking it too far with all that religious stuff. I wasn't going to lie, though. Stacey seemed really sincere and she actually said some things that really made sense. That was rare that I would let someone that went to church all the time talk to me that long about God. They always seemed like they were trying to preach to me, or something. While they would talk I would always think to myself, "I'm not slow, can we have a conversation or something?" They talked as if they were trying to convince *me* that they knew Jesus. What were they trying to prove if they really knew Him? It seemed fake to me.

I didn't think people realized that people who hadn't been in church all of their lives could understand when they heard the truth. There was something about the truth that just sounded right to me. The way Stacey talked about God was different. She talked about Him like He was her best friend, and like they've known each other for years.

"You need to come to my church and stop playin'," Stacey slid in, thinking I wasn't going to notice.

"Uh-huh," was all I said. I wasn't gonna give her no answer that she could hold me to.

Stacey continued to do my hair without pushing the issue about coming to her church. She wasn't too pushy like most people. Most people who went to church all the time got on my damn nerves!

So, I thought that I might just visit her church one of those days. Just maybe.

Chapter 18:
Friends

That night, I refused to be limited to what John considered a good woman to be. I was determined to be my own woman. I was going out with Tre' and no one had to know, including John. I wasn't going to get caught either. B-more, bitch...you know how we do!

I was sexy as shit wit' my black BCBG dress, Gucci purse and black BCBG shoes. I was doin' it semi-casual, but BIG. I had on my Michael Kors perfume and Tre' was ready to eat me up. He *could* eat me as far as I was concerned.

By that time I was getting the hang of sleeping and rolling. Most women tried to act like they were saints. They tried to paint this fantasy picture to men that they had only slept with like two men in their entire lives. I knew the truth. I had only slept with two men and had started having sex in my twenties. Most women I knew had slept with over twenty niggas by the time they were my age but they wouldn't tell it. Especially if they were single and in college—you could forget it!

Things were okay as long as I didn't catch no feelings when it came to having sex. Things were better off when you just got some good dick and then ignored the nigga after it was all over wit'. That way no one got hurt...including me.

Tre' and I went to the first night's show at the Laugh Factory on a Sunday night. We sat upstairs in VIP, watching this comedian by the name of Beth Payne. She had me dyin'! She was sooo funny and animated. She was really pretty too. I know it sounded funny, but I would never have expected someone as pretty as her to be so funny.

Tre' and I were having fun, as usual. I loved going out wit' Tre'. He was so cool. It was going on two weeks since we had slept together, and we had been going out a lot since then. Every chance I got I snuck over to Tre's house. I would always tell John John that I was going out with Trina. He was dumb enough to believe me. I was convinced that men really weren't that smart. Either that or they were so wrapped up in thinking that they were players that they couldn't realize when they were being played.

Everything had moved so fast since John John cheated on me that I didn't have time to think about anything, really. It was best that way. Whenever I even attempted to think about the fact that John just may have raped me, my eyes would well up with tears. Comin' from B-more, you learned how to suck that shit up and move on. That's just how it went. Either survive or be a victim, it was as simple as that.

"Ladies," I could hear Beth Payne say onstage, "you gotta KEEP yo' self.... Keep yo' self!" She was talking about sex. The crowd got quiet for a moment in between their laughs to listen to what she had to say about not having sex. Everyone listened to what she had to say about savin' yourself, and then we were all laughing again when she moved on to her next point.

"Tre'," I asked, looking at him. "Do you think you could wait until marriage to have sex? Could you wait for a woman if you really loved her?"

"Naw," he answered, without putting much thought into it. "We would probably have to get married real quick!"

"So you wouldn't marry a woman without knowing how the sex was?" I felt comfortable asking again. We could talk about anything, so it was cool. I really wanted to know.

"Come to think of it...naw," he said quickly, laughing. "I'm going to be investing too much for me not to know what I'm getting. Don't get me wrong, I don't want no ho, but I definitely ain't feelin' not knowin' what I'm working wit." He laughed and continued. "Shit, if I'm gonna be wit' dat for life, then it better be some good ass pussy!"

"Oh, so you don't want no church girl, huh?" I asked, making jokes.

"Oh, she *needs* to love the Lord. A lot of women in the church don't make you wait that long no way. They *talk* a good game, but eventually they give it up like everyone else—especially if they talkin' to me."

I punched him on the arm as he laughed. He *did* have an effect on women. Every now and again while we were out, I would notice how women would be all up in his face. He never looked back at them when were together, though. He made me feel like I was the only woman that mattered when I went out with him. I don't know what he did when I wasn't around, but when I was around, I was number one.

Before the show ended, Tre' insisted on going to dinner. I didn't mind because I was hungry. We got inside his silver 6-Series BMW coupe and drove down Sunset to get something to eat. The block was mostly empty that night because it was close to nine o'clock on a Sunday.

Tre' pulled out a CD from his case and popped it in. It was Portishead. I loved that group.

"What you know 'bout Portishead?" I asked. I knew that he didn't expect me to know about the group. It was a group over seas that only true music lovers would recognize.

"Okay, ma...I see you," he said smiling at me.

"Tre'," I said, "if I wasn't wit' John, would we be together?"

After I asked, I realized that it was awkward timing. Once we got through the weird silence, Tre' responded, "I'm not ready for a relationship right now, Lady. I know that relationships take a lot of time and energy, and I just can't give that much to one right now. It just wouldn't be fair, I wouldn't want to be selfish like that."

"Oh," I said, not really understanding how he could say that he didn't have that much time when we were always hanging out whenever he wasn't doin' the music thing.

"We **friends** though, right?" Tre' asked.

"Yeah," I responded, instantly thinking about how women would tell me that they were **"friends"** with the man that they were fuckin'. I guessed I'd just joined the club. It didn't make a whole lot of sense, but I was thinking that maybe it was just too soon to be putting labels on it. It was still early, like two weeks. Maybe Tre' would change his mind over time. Plus, I *was* still in a relationship with John John.

In less than five minutes, we pulled up to the Mondrian Hotel where the Skybar was located. A valet opened my door and we went inside. Tre' saw a few people from the industry that he knew. There were a lot of people there for a Sunday night, though. Most people came on a Friday or a Saturday night. I guess everyone had the same idea that night. We walked through the glass doors of the restaurant Asia de Cuba and the hostess sat us at our table. Everything was *real* classy. The waiter came over and took our drink orders and brought some sparkling water back in less than five minutes.

"I hope you don't mind but I invited my boy to come along," Tre' said as he drank his glass of Pellegrino with lemon.

"It's cool," I answered, not minding.

In less than five minutes, his friend walked in and joined us at the table. His friend happened to be one of the largest comedians in the country.

"Lawrence Murphy, this is Lady," Tre' said, introducing me.

"How yew doiiin?" I responded, not seemingly pressed. I never really got too star-struck, maybe because I always considered myself to be a superstar. I figured their breath stank in the morning just like mine.

"Dang, girl!" he laughed. "Where you from?"

"B-more," I said, laughing too. He must have picked up my accent.

"Aight, Aight...I'm from DC," he said proudly.

The waiter came over and asked us for our orders. I knew that at any moment Lawrence was going to start crackin' jokes. I was accustomed to being around comedians. They never stopped the laughs from coming. It's like they would eat, sleep, and breathe it.

I could tell that he was trying to test me out. He looked at me and waited for what seemed like a weak moment so that he could try his best shot at "getting on me." I picked up my napkin and almost knocked over my glass of water in the process. He looked at me, ready to attack.

"Damn, sweetheart...we makin' you nervous?" he asked as he and Tre' laughed. I'm telling you, comedians don't miss a thing.

"Y'all niggas ain't shit," I responded, ready to counter attack.

Lawrence looked at Tre' real hard and his facial expression changed to show that he knew I wasn't no groupie chick.

"Tre', we got a keeper," he smiled at me.

A man walked up with about three women who were nicely dressed. He walked up to Lawrence and shook his hand. I guessed they were joining us too. They all sat at the table and everyone made their introductions.

In less than two minutes, Lawrence started testing them out to see if he could get some jokes out. Just as expected, they were star struck. For the next twenty minutes or so, the table sounded a little bit like this:

"Damn, girl—yo' forehead is huge! Come here, let me use it as a coaster..."

Lawrence had everyone at the table laughing, including the girl he had cracked on. She would just laugh and say, *"So, Lawrence..."* and would continue to question him about his career and his life, as if he hadn't just embarrassed her in front of everyone.

"So, Lawrence..." another woman would say as he would crack on her too.

It was pathetic. I think I heard *"So, Lawrence"* like over thirty times in a matter of twenty minutes. They would sit there and stroke his ego even if he had said, "Hey girl, you ain't nuttin' but a groupie ho." They would just ignore it, laugh and say, *"So, Lawrence."* Lawrence was cool, though. He wasn't into disrespecting women, it was all for fun. But people really tripped off of celebs sometimes. I was seeing the "groupies" in action and was having fun just watching.

The waiter came to the table with our food and I was ready to eat! Tre' had these bomb mashed potatoes with lobster chunks in them. I tore my food up while the other women were being overly prissy. Do you know those heffas wouldn't even eat the bread? Those L.A. women *stayed* on a diet. I was not about to starve foolin' with them.

Ring.

My phone rang and it was Trina. I answered it in case she was trying to tell me that John John was lookin' for me.

"Lady, John John just got locked up," Trina announced.

Chapter 19: Things Done Changed

Things changed once John John got locked up. It had been a month since it all went down. Being that I never got involved in his "business" and he kept me separate from it all, I was clear from being prosecuted. The apartment was in my name, but my truck and other things that we owned were in other people's names. My truck was paid off though. John John had been smart enough to put a certain amount down and triple the payments over a year instead of paying cash for it. No matter how smart and careful John was, he had still gotten himself locked up.

The salon was in the name of one of the barbers from B-more. John's car and other personal things he had were taken. Even though he left me wit' some jewelry I could pawn and some thousands saved up that he hid for hard times, I was left to fend for myself. I wasn't a choreographer yet, so I didn't really make that much money. John John used to make up the difference. Lately, I had been thinkin' 'bout asking

Lord and Trina to help me out by letting me choreograph one of his videos.

Tre' started giving me a couple of thousands here and there and lately he'd been steppin' up his game. That month he paid all my bills, plus he gave me an allowance. Even though we were just "friends", he'd been taking care of me. I was definitely taking care of him. As "inexperienced" as I was, you couldn't tell me I wasn't the shit.

I missed John and I loved him, but I was kinda happy that he wasn't there to control me anymore. I'd been praying and asking God if it was meant for me to be with him. When he got locked up, I took it as a sign that I should start letting him go. Him being locked up was helping, sad to say. I was just used to him taking care of me. It felt kind of good not having to tell someone who I was with, what I was doin', and where I was.

I was on tour dancing with Lord Life, featuring Tre'. Tre' was blowin' up the charts with his first single and Lord's album had already gone platinum. Trina was there to support as usual.

On the night of a show, I was making my way to the bathroom, walking down the hall in a hurry. That night was one of the biggest Awards shows in the African-American community: The AET Awards. That night Tre' was going to perform with Lord Life. Of course I had to do a dance segment. I wasn't really feeling the outfit that I had on. I had on some tacky spandex looking shorts and a cut off top. I knew the eighties style was coming back, but not like that.

As I was walking out of the ladies room, I figured I would go say wassup to Trina since I still had like twenty minutes left before we were up. I walked over to Lord's dressing room and the door was cracked. I pushed it open a little and I saw a reflection of Lord grabbing Trina and literally shaking her. He wasn't beating her but I'd never seen Trina let a man disrespect her like that.

As soon as that happened, I remembered what Tre' said about Lord watching his dad beating his mom's ass and I surely hoped that he wasn't going to do the same thing to Trina. I tried to be positive, being that Lord was pretty calm most of the time. From what I'd seen, he had mad respect for women. He treated women well, unless it was some groupie chick that got on his nerves. He especially treated Trina well. When she walked into the room, she was well taken care of.

I almost thought that he treated women so good because he didn't want to be like his father. I knew by then that, no matter how hard you try, there are certain things that you repeat because you watched your parents do it growing up. Trina probably pissed him off with her little games that she liked to play. I'd have to admit that a lot of them worked, but I didn't know if I'd be going as far as she did.

I pushed open the door when he finally let her go so I could break it up on the low. When they both saw me they acted as if everything was normal. Trina started to walk toward the door.

"Whateva," she said, not even looking at Lord as she walked towards me. "I'm going upstairs." Then she grabbed me to go backstage. "C'mon."

As we walked, I figured I wouldn't be a real friend if I didn't say anything about what I'd just seen.

"Trina, is everything okay with you and Lord? I saw him shaking you through the door."

"Yeah, we aight," she said defensively.

"Are you sure because y'all looked a little intense in there." I tried to say it jokingly to calm things down a little. Trina seemed like she was about to get hostile.

"Look, just because your man cheated on you and got locked up doesn't mean you need to be all up in my shit thinking shit is going on. I *said we aight*!"

"Whatever," I responded, walking away before I slapped the shit out of her. I understood that her man could possibly be beatin' her ass but she didn't have to take it out on me. I was lookin' out for *her*.

I made my way backstage with everyone else. It was five minutes to places.

∎∎∎

I sat with Lord Life and Trina's spoiled ass at one of the tables in the VIP section at Lord's official after party at Aqua nightclub. I was beginning to think that it was his favorite spot to have a party in. It was really nice the way everything was decorated. There were orchid plants everywhere and the ceiling was draped in purple fabric. The theme for the night was "Fit for a King." Lord had become considered one of Hip-Hop's greatest.

It was almost as if I was having dejá vu because Aqua was the first club I'd visited when I first moved to L.A. It had been almost a year and a half.

We sat around the table as I sipped my Midori Sour. I only drank on special occasions. I was still turned off from getting drunk because of my mother. Trina was sitting next to Lord as he entertained one person at a time as they came up to hold a conversation with him. I was wondering where Tre' was, because I was starting to feel like a third wheel sitting there all by myself with only Lord and Trina at the table. Usually John John would be there politicin' wit' Lord while Trina and I would be sitting around talking 'bout people.

Lately, Trina had been acting weird. Even before I saw what happened earlier that day between she and Lord. She was so into the wedding, (that was set for Christmas Eve), that she barely had time to talk like she used to. It seemed to me that all of it was going to her head a little bit. She'd been so wrapped up in Lord Life that it seemed like she was making him her God, or something. She wasn't even trying to go to church as much, which was rare for her.

Finally, Tre' walked up. He wasn't alone.

"Hey, y'all—this is my friend Ebony," he said, introducing this light skinned, petite girl with a long blond and brown weave. She looked aight. Okay, I'm lying...she was real stylish with her Gucci purse that I wanted, and her blue and brown kimono dress.

Trina and I looked at each other and Trina had the nerve to laugh a little bit. She acted like she was getting me back from earlier. She had a look in her eyes that said, "That's what you get." Lord said his "hellos" and proceeded with his conversations. Tre' and Ebony sat at the table next to me. I couldn't believe that shit!

I looked at Tre' because I knew what a "friend" was. So did he think that I was going to be his "friend" while he had other "friends"? The whole "friend" thing was ridiculous. I really knew I was stupid for thinking that maybe he and I were going to be together over time, being that he was taking care of me.

I kept eyeing Tre'. I didn't care if anyone noticed that I was looking.

I looked at him so hard that he looked back at me and said, "What?"

"Let me talk to you for a second," I said, getting up and practically pushing him up with me past his lil' "friend."

We walked outside and stood by the valet.

"Tre'," I said with an attitude. I was ready to hit somebody. "What the fuck is going on?"

"What are you talking about, Lady?" Tre' acted like he was stupid...probably because he was stupid.

"You know what I'm talkin' about! You ain't fuckin' stupid." By that point I had totally lost my cool.

"Lady, like I said before, we are **friends**. We're not together. I wouldn't trip if you'd brought a friend with you tonight."

I looked at him in shock. "Oh really, is that right? So you wouldn't mind if I had sex wit' another nigga, right?" I foolishly thought he would see my point.

"I wouldn't be surprised. You cheated on John to be wit' me, so you probably would fuck some other nigga. Stop trippin', you aint goin' nowhere. You too whipped on this dick."

Tre' got introduced to my fist that night. I wasn't scared of no nigga, so I kept punching him in his face until security came out to break it all up. It wasn't one of those movie slaps, it was one of those punches that you would throw on the streets if a nigga stepped to you wrong. I definitely wasn't concerned with being a Lady at that point. One of the guards grabbed me and held me down as Tre' wiped the drip of blood from his nose. That "star" stuff must have been getting to him too. He must have thought I was going to just let him talk to me like some dumb ass ho. Wrong!

"Consider our friendship over, stupid ass nigga," I shouted as the guard dragged me closer to the parking lot. I pulled away from the guard and fixed my clothes. I was then standing in the parking lot, looking crazy as ever. I gave one of the guys from valet my keys.

I had been through enough of people putting me through changes that night. It was time to go home.

Chapter 20:
Nice Guys
Finish Last

As of the night of the AET awards two weeks before, Tre' and I were over. I'd also quit the tour. I figured I would eventually hurt somebody.

I called the choreographer Shooky Simmons to let him know I was available for work. I decided that I would wait tables and I was starting as a waitress at the Standard on Sunset in two weeks. I didn't care if anyone saw me there either. I would rather take care of myself than to put up wit' niggas tryin' to own me wit' their money.

I just didn't care. I was so fed up that things weren't going *my* way that I decided that I would just treat niggas the way that they treated me.

I had been on the bike at 24 Hour Fitness Workout Gym for about twenty minutes and I was ready to get off. I stared at the TV, waiting for my ten minutes to be over.

I could feel someone staring at me, and I took my eyes off the T.V. screen to meet eyes with a 6'3", dark skinned, cut up, brown-eyed beautiful man using the free weights. He smiled when he noticed that I noticed him looking.

I had no choice but to *roll my eyes back at him*. I wasn't feelin' niggas, so he needed to back off. They all started out big, black and beautiful, but ended up big, black and ugly. Don't get it twisted—I was strictly dickly; I just needed a break.

I looked back at the TV and I could still feel him staring at me. I looked at him again and this time he smiled and waved. Boy, he was persistent. I wasn't falling for that persistent routine again. I half smiled and gave him this fake, "I'm only waving to be polite" wave.

My ten minutes were up and I was happy. It meant I could move to the mats in another location and stretch away from the cutie that was eyeing me down.

As I stretched I remembered the times I used to dance when it was fun. Lately it wasn't that fun anymore. I'd gotten tired of doing the same thing all the time. I wanted something MORE.

Being in L.A. hadn't been all that it was cracked up to be. I didn't mind the hustle, but it was a trip watching how the place could turn people out—including my best friend Trina.

I finished my stretching and walked toward the front door so that I could leave. Of course when I walked outside, the tall handsome man was sitting on the benches using his phone. He got off really quick when he saw me walking and followed me down the escalators.

"Excuse me, lady—may I talk to you for a second?" I could hear a man's voice calling from behind as I walked off the escalators.

I turned around and waited for him to catch up.

"Hi," he said with extra good English. "I'm Louis. Would you mind telling me your name?"

"Lady," I responded.

"No really...what's your name?" he insisted.

"Lady," I responded, with a look that let him know I was serious.

"Beautiful name," he smiled.

Why did he have to have those perfect white teeth?

"Well, it was nice to meet you, Louis." I started to walk away.

"Wait, do you mind if I treat you to a Jamba Juice? I was on my way to get one and I would love for you to join me."

He was so polite. I mean, what did the Negro want? He must've been the brand of player that L.A. produced. "Can I treat you to a Jamba Juice?" Not, "Can we go to dinner?" " Can we catch a movie?" "Can I come over to watch a movie?" (Men in L.A. loved that line.)

"What do you want in return?" I asked, not really caring. "Nothing is free."

"Nothing, I would just like to treat a new friend to a Jamba Juice."

"No thanks," I said, turned off. "I'm not interested in being someone's friend."

I turned around to walk away. He finally left me alone and I decided to go to the music store before I left. I wanted a new CD.

I walked around for about fifteen minutes and got lost in the Broadway Musicals section. Being there took me back to my School for the Arts days when we would perform. I was having fun right there by myself, enjoying the moment.

I looked up and Louis was in the next aisle over. I looked away, hoping that he wouldn't see me. I continued to look at the different CDs, trying to make my decision.

"Can I ask you a question?" a familiar voice said. It was Louis.

"What!?" I outright said.

"Why are you so mean?" he said, smiling. He'd just set himself up for failure.

"Why are you so nice?" I rudely questioned him back.

"I just asked if we could become friends and get to know each other. I didn't ask much."

Did he ever give up?

"Friend, huh?" I was having flashbacks. "So what is a friend?"

He looked at me in a weird and frustrated way and said, "You know what friends are, right? You're kidding, right?"

"Look, I'm not going to waste your time. All you want is a piece of ass. I'm not interested in being your 'friend.' If you want sex, then say it. We're both grown here."

I waited for him to respond to my straightforward comments. I was aware that it was rare for a woman to be that forward. I was tired of playing games.

"Uh, actually I was just interested in being friends. Sorry I wasted your time. Have a blessed evening, sweetheart."

He finally walked off. He had been polite up to his last words. He probably wanted to hit it, anyway.

Chapter 21:
Feenin'

My first day as a waitress was easy money. I surely needed it because I was barely paying rent on time. I didn't really have enough money and it was weighing me down. I wasn't used to being broke.

I hoped that it was the beginning of a life without drama. I had made up my mind that things were going to be done on my terms. If someone didn't like it, then I wasn't dealin' wit' 'em. Period.

The Standard was really trendy with lots of modern decorations everywhere. There were some inside areas and an outside area. The area that I worked in was the diner looking room with booths. It was extremely classy, though. It definitely was not a diner.

I walked over to a new customer who had just been seated. He was a handsome, brown-skinned, business looking type with hazel eyes and sandy brown hair. I stood in front of him ready to take his order. He looked at me in a way that let me know he was interested in me. I was interested too. It had been over a month since I'd last had sex and, to be honest, I was horny.

I had vowed not to get into any relationships. They were just way too complicated and I wasn't feelin' all the games that came along with them. I had just lost my virginity over a year ago and I was really frustrated at that point. If I'd had it my way, I would have stayed with one person for the rest of my life. Things just don't work out that way.

I was just a little angry at the fact that every woman around me who was a ho and treated men like dirt was getting those men to treat them like they were a queen. I probably just should have stayed single and a virgin for the rest of my life. Now I was single and horny. Not a nice combination. Not at all.

After I finished taking the handsome man's order, I went over to the computer to put the order in. I knew he was looking at me while I was punching everything in. That entire night he studied me.

Finally, when I brought him his check he said, "What time do you get off? You wanna go for some drinks?"

"How about what's your name?" I asked, staring him in the eyes.

"You look like a woman that's to the point," the handsome man replied. "I figured if you said 'yes' to drinks then I would naturally get your name later."

"Very good observation," I said, without any facial expression. "I get off in ten minutes."

It was early evening and the night wasn't anywhere near being over.

"Here's my cell number," he said as he wrote down his number. "And my name is Dennis. From Morgan State, remember?"

I looked at him really good but I didn't remember him from my old college.

"No."

He went in his pocket and pulled out his glasses. He put them on.

"Wait," I said, changing my mind. "You were an engineering major! Dennis, *oh my God*! Look at you!"

"Hurry up and get out of here so we can catch up," he said smiling.

I got my things together, met with my manager then walked over to the table where Dennis was sitting. Dennis and I walked out of the Standard on Sunset and we just talked about the good ol' days back at Morgan. We decided that we were having fun just walking, so we didn't go out for drinks.

I found out that Dennis was in L.A. on business and was in town for only two weeks. He was an engineer and had traveled for work while also using the time for some vacation. He seemed really happy about his career choice. I knew his pockets were happy too!

He told me who was at homecoming that year and how everyone was starting to look different already. We laughed so hard, talking about folks who had graduated. It was so good to talk to someone from college again. We walked back and forth for at least an hour. It was a pretty chilly night and I had on my jacket. I was ready to go.

"I don't know about you but I'm tired," Dennis said, looking really sleepy. I'm staying right at the W Hotel over by UCLA. You are more than welcome to hang out, no pressure."

"Sure," I said, without thought. I knew what time it was.

We walked back to the Standard, got our cars from the valet and I followed Dennis back to his hotel. We drove down Sunset to get there, past Beverly Hills. Every time I drove past Beverly Hills I admired how the palm trees were perfectly lined up and down the street. It was also crazy how the fire hydrants and the street signs were silver. I just couldn't get over that.

We pulled up to the valet in front of the W Hotel and got out so one of the gentlemen could park our cars. The steps at the W were clear and they had water running down them. I walked with Dennis up those water filled steps. Then he grabbed my hand and pulled me toward the elevators.

We walked to his room and he had a suite with a small office. It was the standard W Hotel room. It was nice.

"So," I asked, sitting in his office chair, "why aren't you in a relationship? Or are you?"

"I just started my career so I'm not really looking," he responded, answering the question he had expected I would ask him.

"So...if you're not interested in a relationship, then why are you talking to me?" I wanted to get to the meat of things.

"Well, I thought it would be good to meet up with an old friend. Plus, I'm single, you're single — we're not hurting anyone by having a good time."

"*Right*. So you're only here for two weeks and you don't want a relationship right now. *Hmmm*. Let's be real - why are you talking to me right now?" I was digging deeper for the truth.

"Because you're beautiful," he answered effortlessly. I enjoy being in the company of beautiful women like yourself."

I thought to myself, "Why can't men just be real and say what they want? It would make life a lot easier that way. Just tell the freakin' truth." I got up and sat next to Dennis on the bed.

"Dennis," I said, "just be real." You don't want a relationship and you're only here for two weeks. You just want to fuck, admit it." I was looking at him right in his eyes. "Tell the truth, in case we both want the same thing."

"Okay," he said, more than surprised with the little commentary I'd just made. "I want to have sex."

"Me too," I said, looking him in his face. His facial expression changed and he was shocked.

That was the first night that I began to know what I wanted and how to get things done MY way. That was the beginning of me living a single life without me owing anybody anything.

I had been **feenin'** that night and the need was fulfilled. We were both happy. We both got some really great sex and I didn't stalk him down like some crazy woman. If anything, he called me everyday while he was in L.A. and then still kept calling me when he left. I wasn't trying to catch feelings and I explained that he shouldn't either.

I just wanted to hit.

Chapter 22:
The devil
Does Exist

I was making just enough by dancing and waiting on tables. I was stubborn and I took money from whoever I was messin' wit' only when I had to. I was so turned off by how Tre' and John John had acted that I refused to let a nigga think that he could buy me. I could see what Trina meant when she used to tell me that a man would try to own you with his pockets.

I had been single for six months and I was "gettin' some" at least every week. I would never screw the same man more than once, but I was definitely gettin' it in. I could see how most women lied about how many men they'd been wit'. I was definitely lying too. That information was not up for discussion. As far as I was concerned, if I only slept with someone one time then it didn't count. And if the sex was wack or he came in less than three minutes, then that *definitely* didn't count. After I took all of that into consideration, I was still under the average number of partners that most women had been with. I wondered how many men Trina had been wit' by then. Like twenty?

The closer it got to Trina and Lord's wedding the less I spoke to her. We would talk here and there but she was really wrapped up in everything. She finally told her parents and they had a fit, of course. They had no choice but to get over it. Trina was determined that she was getting married in December. She claimed she was in love.

Deep down inside, I wasn't really happy. I truly longed to be in a committed relationship but niggas were just crazy. Every nigga wanted a "friend" and they expected women to just wait until they got ready to commit. I wasn't feelin' that concept. I made things less complicated by just "getting some" and going 'bout my business.

I arrived at Stacey's birthday 'get together' at her house and pulled up into her driveway. She lived in Foxhills—a really expensive area, mostly condos, where a lot of black professionals lived. I heard that some ball players stayed there from time to time. I walked up to her building and looked for the name Stacey Cooper on the roster.

"Hey, Stacey - it's me, Lady," I said. I talked to Stacey through the speaker outside the main entrance.

"Alright," she replied. "Just come up and go to the right. My door will be open."

I walked in her condo and it was really pretty. She had it decorated really nicely. She had a burnt orange accent wall and light blue sofa with color accent pillows. She was really classy. There were about twenty people in her home. Everyone was sitting around talking. She had some gospel music on and it sounded kinda *aight*. It was like some gospel rap & gospel R&B—but it definitely didn't sound corny. Her home had a certain calmness about it. I felt relaxed as soon as I walked in.

"Hey, Lady!" Stacey said, walking over to me. "Thanks for coming girl!"

"Thanks for the invite," I said.

"Make yourself at home," she offered.

I sat down on the sofa and talked to some people here and there. I was actually having some fun. The food was good too. Stacey could really cook. I don't think she could've beaten me in the kitchen, though. I was tough competition.

We stayed up playing board games and group games. My stomach hurt from laughing so much.

Time flew until it was eleven at night. Mostly everyone had left to go home and it was only me, Stacey, and about four of Stacey's friends. We sat on the floor and the sofa, having a deep conversation about life. Naturally, we started talking about God.

They all talked about how living life as a Christian was hard but it was worth it. They then talked about how it was better to live under the protection of God.

"Yeah, I'm thankful man," Stacey said to everyone. "God protects us from a lot. He is so good, he even protects us from the things we don't see."

"Yeah, I know that's right!" someone else added in.

"Like right now, there's spiritual warfare going on," Stacey continued. "There are angels around protecting us."

This petite brown skinned lady by the name of Brooke spoke up and said, "Yeah. I remember when I was scared to get saved at first because every time I would get close to God it seemed like I would start seeing demons."

"You can see demons?" I asked. I started to get cold. This was the part where I would talk about God and things would get really weird. "You weren't scared?"

"Heck yeah, at first," Brooke responded. I used to cry at night because I couldn't get a peaceful night's sleep. But then I learned how powerful the name of Jesus is when you say it and believe. I started calling on Him, and I stopped being afraid."

I was getting even colder. By that time I couldn't stop shaking. Every time I was around a conversation about demons, I would just shake uncontrollably. I felt like as long as I prayed every night and didn't try to get all serious about God then I didn't have to deal with all that demonic stuff. The more everyone stayed on the subject the more uncomfortable I became.

"That's why I can't play with God," another person said. It's not a game man, for real."

"You aren't afraid?" I asked everyone.

"The one thing that you fear is the one thing that's blocking your true gifts *and* your true purpose," Stacey responded. "There is no fear in

Jesus Christ. That's the reason why I ain't half crazy today!"

"Yes girl," Brooke added. "Sometimes I see that demon that a person might be dealing with and that lets me know how to pray for them. Plus it keeps me in check and gives my hardheaded butt more motivation to obey God. He's the one who fights my battles. I wouldn't be able to pray for someone correctly if I was out there doing who knows what."

"S-s-s-s-o people have d-d-demons that they are d-d-dealing with?" I said, shaking even harder.

"Yeah!" Stacey said. "It may be a demon of lust, a demon of pride, a demon of loneliness, or whatever a person can't seem to stop doing that is against God's word. Usually there's some demonic force tryin' to hide behind some human, causing them to do things that end up leading them to destruction. You'd be surprised."

"Yeah," Brooke said. "The truth is, *things that you don't see are more real than the things that you do see*. Demons are real, but God is real too. That's why you have to stay close to him. It ain't no joke out here."

I really started to shake from ongoing chills. It wasn't like a coldness that you would feel outside on a winter's day. There was "coldness" deep down in my gut that made the hair on my body stand up. The chill was inside of me. Outside was warm; I was the only one shaking in the room.

"So j-j-just because you can't *see* d-demons, they may still be there?" I asked.

"Of course," Brooke said, talking freely and not being bothered by our topic of discussion. "Everyone isn't blessed to see them. If they were, half the people out here wouldn't do half the things they do. They really wouldn't do it if they really knew who and what was in charge of it all."

I felt the presence of something go past me. I couldn't see anything. My teeth started to chatter. The room felt like it was closing in on me the more we talked about demonic forces.

"So what is the d-demon of lust in charge of?" I asked.

"Usually sexual sins," Stacey said.

My mind raced. Everyone's words started to blur together. I remembered when I was a little girl. I remembered when I was twelve and I would sit up with my friends reading the Bible until it got late. I remembered telling God that I was going to wait until I was married to have sex. I remembered someone telling me that it was unrealistic for me to wait. I thought about how many people I had slept with and how I was angry because every man I had messed with had broken my heart.

I just couldn't take it anymore. I started to feel even colder and shake even harder than before. This time I couldn't just change the subject and act like something wasn't going on inside of me.

"Raaaaaaaaaaaaaaaaaaaaaaaaaaaaaaaa!!!!!!!!!!"
I started screaming to the top of my lungs at a

really high pitch and I couldn't stop. My face was scrunched up in order to get the scream out. I couldn't stop screaming.

"JESUS...the blood of Jesus..." I could hear someone saying.

I kept screaming even more loudly.

"Jesus...the blood of Jesus," I could hear people saying. "In the name of Jesus. Jesus....the blood of Jesus. Jesus...Jesus..."

I had never told anyone, but the one thing I feared was getting close to God and having to deal with demons. It seemed like I could feel the presence of them sometimes. As long as I wasn't trying to get close to God then I wouldn't feel them as much.

I started to cry uncontrollably.

I could hear Stacey's voice somewhere in the midst of the screaming saying, "...**He who dwells in the secret place of the most high shall rest and abide in the shadow of the almighty. I will say of the Lord. He is my refuge and my fortress. My God in whom I trust...**"

"In the name of Jesus...Jesus...Jesus..." I could hear people saying while Stacey was talking.

"**Surely he shall deliver thee from the snare of the fowler, and from the noisome pestilence. He shall cover thee with thy feathers and under thy wings shall thou trust. His truth shall be they shield and buckler....**"

"Jesus...Jesus..." I kept hearing everyone say while Stacey was saying what sounded like a scripture out of the Bible.

My body laid still. Finally, the coldness was gone. I stopped shaking. I stopped screaming. My face wasn't scrunched up anymore. I just cried.

"Praise you God, thank you Jesus..." I could hear everyone saying. They all continued. "Hallelujah Lord. You're *worthy* Lord. THANK YOU LORD. You are so awesome." They were so excited and some people were in tears.

One person was laid out on the floor praying, while Brooke was walking around clapping her hands.

Stacey was bowed over with her hands spread out at both of her sides saying, "Thank you Jesus! You're worthy!" Stacey started to jump up and down, praising God.

I just sat there with tears in my eyes. I couldn't really move. I'd never experienced anything like that before. I just broke down and cried.

When everyone got quiet and went back to talking, I made an announcement.

"I would like to get saved," I said, surprising myself. "I did it when I was eight, but can I do it again, just to make sure? Do I have to wait until I go to church?"

"Of course...yes...Praise God..." I could hear everyone saying at different times.

I was tired of running away. I had run away from my family issues and I had been running away from God. I was tired.

I wasn't happy with how I had been living my life. Not only did it make me stressed out, but

I was also lonely, depressed, heart-broken, and scared. I was ready for a change. I noticed that I had tried not to repeat the same mistakes that my parents had made but I found myself making them anyway. Even though I had dealt with men who seemed like they were protecting me at first, they had turned on me. I felt like I was out there alone, and at that moment I needed some real protection. After that night, the name of Jesus didn't seem like a bad idea.

"You can always dedicate your life to God again," Brooke announced. "You can do it now. You don't have to wait to go to church."

Stacey grabbed her Bible and read:

"If you confess with your mouth 'Jesus is Lord', and believe in your heart that God raised him from the dead, you will be saved."

"That was Romans 10:9," Stacey said. "Do you believe that Jesus is Lord, and do you believe in your heart that God raised him from the dead?" Stacey asked.

" I believe that Jesus is Lord, and I believe that God raised him from the dead," I responded.

"Say 'I confess'," Stacey said.

"I confess," I repeated. I continued to repeat these words:

"Everything I did in my past that displeased God was sin. I repent of it. I renounce it. I plead the blood of Jesus that washes out all sin and iniquity. Lord, I choose to live for you from this day forward. I want a personal relationship with Jesus Christ."

"Then you are saved," Stacey said, smiling.

"We're here if you have questions," Brooke added while she hugged me.

"Being saved is about a personal relationship with Jesus," Stacey said. "Get to know him by reading His word. The Bible has almost every answer to life's questions. You're not alone. You can trust God. Girl, consider *Him* to be 'yo' Daddy'! It's all good...I'm tellin' you!"

Everyone came around and hugged me.

■■■

That night, I couldn't really sleep much. Stacey let me stay on her sofa. I refused to go home and sleep by myself. I felt more comfortable at her house. Just in case something jumped off, I would be near someone. I knew I wasn't supposed to fear, but everything was so new to me. All I knew was there was something about calling on the name of Jesus.

I looked around the room. It was quiet. Nothing was going on.

I told Stacey that I would go to church with her the next day. She stayed up with me for as long as she could. Eventually, she pulled out a night-light from a drawer in her kitchen and plugged it in for me. She went to bed, not even bothered by what had just happened.

Me, I kept one eye closed and the other one open. I finally drifted off to sleep after my eyes got tired of looking around. I slept, holding the Bible.

Part Two:
A.D.

Chapter 23:
YES!

Singing.
"Jesus, I'll never forget what you done fo' me. Jesus, I'll never forget how you set me freeeee. Jesus, I'll never forget, how you brought me out. Jesus, I'll never forget…noooo neeeeeever."

I walked into Tabernacle of Praise Worship Center with Stacey, wearing the same clothes I'd had on the night before. Stacey and I didn't wear the same size, and everything I'd tried of hers didn't fit. She insisted that no one was going to care about my clothes and that it wasn't that type of church. But everyone was *dressed*. Any other day I would have felt out of place with my wrinkled clothes, but that day I just wanted to go to church. All I cared about was being safe and getting to God as soon as possible.

"I won't forget…I won't forget…no neeeeevvvaaaa!" A light-skinned, well-dressed, energized young man sang on the mic. He was pumped up about singing the song. Everyone was

really excited right along with him. I couldn't lie, so was I.

I sat down while everyone else stood up, clapping their hands and stomping their feet. The first thing I noticed about the church was that it was different. Everyone seemed really serious about praise and worship. They weren't just clapping their hands and singing a song. It seemed like everyone there had his or her own story and reason for getting pumped up. Some people were crying. Some people were dancing. Some people had to jump up and down in the middle of the song. It didn't seem like they cared if anyone was looking at them, just as I didn't care if anyone was looking at me in my busted up outfit. I wasn't even mad when a guy jumped up and ran around the church. After the night before, I wanted to run too. I'd heard that calling on Jesus was the best thing to do. That night, I had seen it for myself.

All I knew was that I wanted more, and I wanted to get to a place where Jesus didn't mind being there. Stacey insisted that her church was different. People there weren't perfect, but everyone there was striving for perfection. She said that you could actually see a change in people from the first time they had started going there. On the way to church, Stacey shared with me that she wasn't always saved. **She even had her story**.

Tabernacle of Praise was a small church that sat about two hundred people. A lot of the members seemed to be around my age, even though there were a lot of older people as well.

Who knows, everyone looked young in L.A. for the most part. To be honest, I really didn't care. It was the first day that I wanted to be open to what God was going to say and not be worried about people. I just wanted to hear from God.

A young man stood and said, "Everybody stand on your feet as I present to you our pastor, Elder David A. Rhone!"

Everyone stood up, excited that the pastor was getting up to preach. He took his place at the podium, with probably more excitement than everyone in the church put together, and I could tell that he was going to have a lot of energy.

"PRAISE THE LORD, everybody!!!" Pastor Rhone said with a tone of authority and anticipation. "C'mon, I said PRAISE THE LOOORD EVERRRYBODYYY!!!!! I need about twenty-five hand clappers! Where are my hand clappers..."

The entire church stood up and starting praising God again. That church seemed like they never got tired of praising God. They weren't playing up in there.

"I need you to turn to your neighbor and say, 'Things are getting better in my life.' I need you to say it...look the person next to you in their eyes and say it like you really mean it! Every morning when I wake up, I tell myself that things are getting better in my life! And it IS so!"

The pastor encouraged everyone for a good ten minutes. He acted as if he never got tired. I started to feel a little better. I had barely gotten any sleep the night before. I kept trying to look around in case anything "popped" up. Stacey told me that I shouldn't fear, but that was easier said than done. But she gave me some type of hope. Seeing that she wasn't afraid after what had happened the night before amazed me. She'd just gone to sleep like nothing had happened.

"I want everyone to turn to John, the fourteenth chapter," the pastor said. "I want to preach to you just a few minutes this morning. When you have the word of the Lord, I want you to jump to your feet and I want you to look at verses one through six."

Stacey and I stood up. I watched Stacey turn right to the scripture, and she let me hold the Bible with her so that we could share.

"And I want to conclude at verse twenty-seven," the pastor continued. "The Lord has re-routed me just a little bit this morning, and I will pick up on our Series of Purpose on Wednesday night. I want to encourage your hearts this morning as we prepare to give what God has given us. When you have the word, I want you to shout and say, *'I've got the word!'* The Bible says…"

We read in our Bibles:

"Do not let your hearts be troubled. Trust in God. Trust in me also. There are many rooms in my Father's house. If this were not true, I would have told you. I am going there to prepare a place for you. If I go and do that, I will come back. And I will take you to be with me. Then you will also be

where I am. You know the way to the place where I am going. Thomas said to him, 'Lord, we don't know where you are going. So how can we know the way?' Jesus answered, 'I am the way and the truth and the life. No one comes to the Father except through me."

"Flip over to twenty-seven," the pastor continued. We read:

"I leave my peace with you. I give my peace to you. I do not give it to you as the world does. Do not let your hearts be troubled. And do not be afraid. You heard me say, 'I am going away. And I am coming back to you.' If you loved me, you would be glad I am going to the Father. The Father is greater than I am. I have told you now before it happens. Then when it does happen, you will believe."

"I feel like shouting right now!" the pastor said, right after reading. "Jesus is saying, 'While you're in it, I'm already telling you how you're coming out!' You better look at somebody and tell them, 'I already know how I'm comin' out!' Y'ALL DON'T WANNA HELP ME IN HERE!!!!! Look at somebody and say, 'I already know how I'm COMIN' OUT!'"

Pastor Rhone wouldn't stop until everyone was as excited as he was about what he was saying. I thought about everything going on in my life and it wasn't easy to say those words. The night before had seemed like it wouldn't end. I was hoping that everything was going to be okay. Pastor Rhone went on.

"Look at your neighbor before you take your seat this morning and say, 'Neighbor, everything is gonna be alright!' You don't know what the person next to you is going through. Lay your hands on your neighbor standing next to you and tell em', 'Whatever you're going through, the Lord wants you to know that everything is gonna be alright!" Pastor Rhone spoke with confidence. "Now, if you believe, clap your hands and give God the praise. *I said if you believe it*; clap your hands! I SAID, IF YOU BELIEVE IT, clap your hands and give God the praise!"

"Hallelujah!!" people around me were saying. Pastor Rhone kept preaching.

"Now take your seats in the presence of the Lord. Now as I preach to you this morning, I want you to understand that while you're in whatever you're in, you already have a voice that says you're coming out of it. Y'all don't wanna *hear* me this morning! I said, you hear a voice that says YOU'RE COMING OUT OF IT! And you're coming out with victory!"

"Hallelujah!!" people kept saying. "Thank you Jesus!"

It was as if God was speaking to me himself. To be honest, I was scared. I wasn't sure what to do from that point on. Sure, I could call on Jesus, but would he respond to me like he'd responded to everyone who was at Stacey's house the night before? I wasn't going to shout 'Hallelujah!' and act like I really believed in what the pastor was saying.

Sure, I believed in God, but it was all a bit much for me at that moment. First I had realized that my dad wasn't as perfect as I thought he was. Then I realized that I wasn't going to be with John John for the rest of my life. He wasn't perfect, just like my father wasn't perfect. John John was all I'd really had out in L.A.

I had closed up and had started sleeping with men without any commitments, without even caring anymore. Yeah, I knew it may not have been right, but when I tried to do the right thing I got cheated on, raped, abused, lied to, disrespected, and robbed of my feelings even more. The more I had tried to get closer to God, the more I felt the presence of something that wouldn't let me get close to God without a fight. It was too much pressure and I wanted to break down. I wasn't even sure if I wanted to get close to God after all of that. All I knew was that I wanted whatever was going on to stop. A warm tear ran down my face.

Pastor kept teaching. "But I want you to understand where Jesus is in the text. When you study John thirteen, fourteen, fifteen, sixteen, and seventeen, you understand that Jesus is now preaching his last discourse. Jesus is at the last supper and he is giving his last will and testament before he dies on the cross."

I didn't completely understand what he was talking about. I remembered the last supper and everything from Sunday school when I used to go, but I was starting to wonder where the pastor was going with all of it.

He continued. "I want you to understand the tone of the atmosphere during this time in the Bible. When Jesus got closer to dying on the cross, the atmosphere was very solemn. The atmosphere was very depressing. The atmosphere was very heavy…"

I could certainly relate to all of that. I felt like I was almost at my lowest. Honestly, I was tired. I kept listening to the pastor's words.

"Jesus is explaining to his disciples that I am about to die a horrific death and there is nothing that can be done about it. And *you've* got to understand that in the midst of the challenges of life that there are going to be things that crop into your life that you have no control over. *I wish I had a witness!* But in the midst of a situation that is on its way to being emotionally out of control, Jesus steps on the scene and reels it back in place. Now it's very solemn, because the disciples are feeling the anxiety of everything that's about to happen. Jesus is about to be taken from them and they don't understand the 'why' of what's going on. *There are times in your life when you don't understand the 'why' of what's going on.* But Jesus now tells his disciples in the midst of this situation, 'Let not your heart be troubled.' Now, when I look at the word 'trouble' in Greek it means 'tarasso', or to agitate. It means inward commotion. It means to take away the calmness out of your mind. It means to make restless. It means to strike one's spirit with fear and dread. It means to be anxious or to be distressed. It means to be perplexed or confused in your mind, suggesting doubt and unbelief. WHEN you are troubled, you don't see a way out. WHEN you are troubled, you are confused and uncertain about the future. WHEN you are troubled, you don't have answers to many questions. WHEN you are troubled, there is uneasiness in your spirit. But Jesus is telling the disciples that where they are — and he's giving them a command, not a request — there are some things in your life where you just have to walk in the commands of the Lord. Lay your hands on your neighbor and say, 'Where I am in my life, I've got to live by the commands of the Lord."

Stacey looked at me and repeated what the pastor had said. The more the pastor preached, the more it seemed as though God was speaking directly to me. I didn't know if I could handle it all. I wasn't sure if I was ready to live the Christian life or if I could really do it. I had already been a failure up to that point and hardly knew the Bible. I really didn't know for myself what God considered to be right and wrong. I focused back on the pastor.

"Now the Lord is saying, 'I knows there's anxiety in your spirit. I know there's uncertainty about what's about to happen.' But Jesus says, 'Let not your heart be troubled — JUST BELIEVE!' And see there comes a time in your life where you are going to have to come out of your reality and stand flat-footed and say, 'I believe God.' Jesus says don't be troubled and just believe. Don't worry about how you're gonna get the job—just believe! Don't worry about the chaos and hell in your family—just believe! Don't worry about the health challenges in your body—just believe! Don't worry about the MADNESS in your reality—JUST BELIEVE! Somebody shout, 'Just believe!' I said shout, 'Just believe!'"

"Believe, just believe..." the church was saying in bits and pieces all around the building.

"To believe means to be persuaded," the pastor preached. "To believe means to be convinced. To believe means to credit with verity and trust that there's a guarantee of a present reality. When I AM A BELIEVER, I am *persuaded* that things will work out in my favor!"

Even though I had just rededicated my life to God the night before, I was starting to wonder if I was truly the believer that the pastor talked about. Honestly, I wasn't sure how everything was going to turn out. I wasn't sure if I would be able to handle what had happened on the night before by myself if no one was around. At that point I figured out that I didn't know much of anything. I just knew that God had some better answers than what I was coming up with.

The pastor shouted, "I am talking about a confident assurance BASED on the word of GOD that things are about to change and get better! Jesus is saying DON'T WORRY ABOUT IT—just believe what I tell you. Now saints, where you are in your life right now, the devil is *trying* to run you mad…"

I knew the pastor had to be talking to me. More tears escaped the corners of my eyes. My body started to warm up.

"The devil is trying to run you crazy," he continued. "I WISH I HAD A WITNESS! The devil is trying…O God…to make you think that because of the hell in your reality, that all you can expect is hell in your future. So you're really not expecting anything in your future, because you are so heavy laden with your reality. But your reality and your future ain't got nothing to do with one another. *I wish somebody would help me!* I said your reality and your future ain't got nothing to do with one another. Now, the command is not 'be troubled', but to believe. Now what Jesus is saying is that what you believe has the power to overpower your reality…*y'all don't wanna have church wit' me today!* I said…the command is that what you believe has the power to overcome *everything* that's pressing and weighing you down. You have to understand that WHAT I believe has the power…O, God…to overturn my present reality. WHAT I believe has the power to turn my unemployment into employment. WHAT I believe has the POWER to turn defeat into victory! WHAT I believe has the power…O, God…to take things working against me and turn them into working for me. WHAT I believe has the power to shut down EVERY system, *shut down EVERY DEVIL*, and allow victory and overcoming to flow in my life! WHAT I believe has the power to shut down every negative force and allow me to live in the possibility in my future. O saints, you've got to understand that your belief is more than just a clapping of the hands and a stomping of the feet. But what I believe is an assurance in my spirit that what God spoke over my life is about to happen, and I'm expecting it any time now…"

So far God had promised me that I was going to be okay, that he would protect me and never leave me. That's all I cared about. It was hard for me to trust God, who I couldn't see, to keep his word; people who I saw every day abandoned me and hurt me. As soon as I trusted someone, they turned on me. The pastor went on.

"I want you to look at your neighbor and tell them that everything is going be alright! Tell them again, and say that everything is going to BE alright! The pastor responded to my thoughts and to the entire congregation.

Stacey looked at me and spoke those words, and I realized that what the pastor was saying must be true. Stacey was proof that everything was going to be alright. She told me that she used to be so scared that she had to sleep with a night-light, and that the only reason she was scared was because she wasn't living her life according to the word of God. She didn't have confidence in what God could do because she really didn't believe that everything that God said was true. Stacey revealed that it wasn't until she found out how "real" God was for herself that she had been able to stand on her own two feet in the confidence of what God says. Looking at her, looking at how she'd handled the night before and at how she lived her life, gave me a glimpse of hope. The pastor was still excited.

"The command is that no matter how DARK it is, *just BELIEVE!* Jesus says, 'Now the promise is that I go to prepare a place for you.' Jesus says that 'I leave you in your present reality, but I'm leaving to go get stuff ready for you.' See saints, when you live by your reality, you have no expectation. When you live by your reality, there is no hope. But when you do like the Bible says, it says that *'the just shall live by faith.'* I'm not living my life by what I see, but I'm living my life based on what God spoke to me. When you walk by faith, you're walking and believing God about invisible things that are going to manifest. When you walk by faith, you're living your life based upon what God tells you. There are no details. There are no explanations. It's just, 'This is what God said to me.' Well, you say, 'Pastor, that's living my life in uncertainty.' No, it's not! See, you've got to understand that **THE THINGS YOU DON'T SEE ARE MORE REAL THAN THE THINGS YOU DO SEE!**"

That statement reminded me of what had happened the night before. I knew something was going on and I was in trouble, but I couldn't see anything. I could just feel it. And when they called on the name of Jesus, he had to have been there, even though I didn't see Him. I knew last night that some invisible force was helping me.

"Oh, y'all don't want to hear me today," the pastor kept preaching. *"I said the things you can't see are more real than the things you can see*! If you can just learn to live your life based on the promises of God, then you'll NEVER be defeated. Somebody shout, 'Praise the Lord'!"

"Praise the Lord!" different people shouted.

I mustered up enough energy to say 'Praise the Lord' as I sat in my seat, getting even warmer the more the pastor preached. I started to cry, realizing that I hadn't really been living to please God as much as I'd should've. I began to wonder if that was why I was so run down and tired. I was so tired.

"Jesus says to the disciples," the pastor continued, " 'I KNOW you're exhausted and I KNOW you're drained. But he says don't be troubled and just believe.' He says, 'I go to prepare a place for you that where I am, you will be there too.' So the Lord has promised them about preparation for something better. The Lord has promised them a phenomenal future. God is saying, 'I know that you're in a mess, but I AM preparing something better for you.' I KNOW it's a little dark right now, but the WORD of the Lord to you in THIS place today is that preparations are being made for phenomenal futures! Look at your neighbor and tell them that 'God has prepared a phenomenal future for me.' I SAID, look at your neighbor right in their face and say 'God has prepared a phenomenal future for me.'"

I looked at Stacey and she looked at me and we kept saying it to each other. The pastor told us to repeat it at least five times. The more I said those words, the more I began to cry. I felt like something was being released the more I repeated those words.

"See," the pastor said, "The more you say it, the more it gets in your spirit and the devil can't shake it! *You better look behind you and tell your neighbor that* 'GOD has prepared a phenomenal future for me!' See, every time you say it, you defy what you're in right now! Look at somebody else and say, 'GOD has prepared a phenomenal—I didn't say mediocre, I didn't say no half thing—but a PHENOMENAL future!!!! See, Jesus wants us to understand that the reason that we are going to make it is because of our union with the Father. You have to understand that the way has already been made. Jesus says, 'I am the WAY, the TRUTH, and the LIFE.' He says, 'If you believe God, then you've got to believe in me as well, because God and I are the same.' Philippians says, 'If you show us the Father, then we'll be satisfied.' Jesus says, 'I've been with you all this time, and don't you understand that if you have seen me, then you have seen the Father.'

I kept thinking about the night before and how the name of Jesus changed the entire situation. I didn't fully understand how Jesus was God, but I knew for sure that the name of Jesus was powerful. At that point I believed that he was God, since it said it in the Bible. I knew the word of God had to be real.

"And Jesus says," the pastor emphasized, "'I'm going to prepare a great future for you.' And you've got to believe your future, even though you don't see it yet. You've got to understand that if you have faith of what's to come....O, God…then you can have power to go through the hell that's just temporary in your life. See, you've got to understand that where you are now IS NOT where you're *always* going to be."

I was surely hoping that I wasn't always going to be scared to go home and go to sleep. Right then it just seemed like I wasn't going to be able to get past all of it. All I wanted to do was get closer to God. I was tired of running away. I kept crying, thinking about growing up with my alcoholic mother and how it had just became normal to me. That's just how it was. I became hard in order to survive in my house and survive growing up in Baltimore. I could look right in the eyes of someone who was trying to kill me and not be moved. The only thing that could faze me was what had happened the night before. That night, *I couldn't even see* what was trying to mess with me. I wondered how I was going to survive it all.

Pastor Rhone went on, "Now the only way you gonna make it out of the trouble of the world is with the help of the Holy Spirit." I sat in my chair, amazed at how God was speaking directly to me. The pastor continued. "But in this chapter, Jesus promises them…the Holy Spirit. He says he's leaving as a physical man, but he's coming back as the eternal spirit—and the Holy Spirit is the spirit of Christ. The Bible says that the Holy Spirit has been called alongside to help. The Holy Spirit is more than just a jerk, more than a clapping of the hands...the Holy Spirit is the spirit of Christ that is called alongside to help me. There is a trial in your life where you think you're not going to be able to make all by yourself; there is a TRIAL in your life where you think that the devil is gonna try to kill you over! BUT I, I'm GOIN' TO MAKE IT because I..." the Pastor began to shout to the top of his lungs "...I GOT THE HOLY GHOST!!!!!! I said that the Holy Ghost is my helper, MY STRENGTH! "

I thought back to when I was baptized when I was twelve. Even though I really wanted to live for God back then, I'd walked away. I wasn't even sure if I understood what I was doing. I wasn't sure if I even had the Holy Spirit. I didn't even feel like God was with me anymore.

"There is a trial that will make you turn back from God," Pastor Rhone said. "That will make you say, 'Lord. I can't take the pressure. I can't take the heat.' But when you understand the power of the Holy Spirit...the Holy Spirit is my intercessor...*don't sleep* on the POWER of the Holy Spirit! I hear the Lord say in Romans, chapter eight, that 'the Spirit itself bears witness with my spirit and it will identify that I am a son of God.' I hear the Lord say that 'if any man does not have the Spirit of Christ then he is none of his! Look at somebody and tell them, 'Neighbor, you've got to have the Holy Ghost!"

When Stacey turned to me, she made me cry even more. I needed God in my life. Even though people had turned me off from wanting to be with him, I really needed to find out about him for myself. I was desperate. I didn't know anyone or anything else that could help me. I was hurt, barely paying my bills, lonely, confused, and bitter. And now, I was one step away from going crazy. I was so tired...

"How you goin' to make it if you don't have the Holy Ghost?" the pastor asked. "It's because of the Holy Ghost that I'm still here with expectation. It's because of the Holy Ghost inside, telling me that I'm going to make it! Yes, Lord! I, I'm SO GLAD, SO GLAD, SO GLAD that I've got the Holy Ghost!"

I cried to God in my mind so that only God could hear. "Lord," I said. "I need you. I can't do this by myself anymore..."

The pastor continued. "You've got to understand that the Holy Ghost is the sealer of your future. It's because of the Holy Ghost that I'll be called up when the trumpet sounds. I DON'T KNOW WHAT'S WRONG WITH Y'ALL, but I'm not ashamed OF THE HOLY GHOST! Lift your hands and say 'LORD, I THANK YOU FOR THE HOLY GHOST!' AND IF YOU DON'T HAVE IT, YOU NEED TO GET IT! SHOUT HALLELUJAH, SHOUT HALLELUJAH! DO YOU REMEMBER WHEN GOD FILLED YOU WITH HIS SPIRIT? Don't mess wit' me! I'm 'bout to start shoutin'! Ask your neighbor, 'DO YOU REMEMBER THE FIRST TIME YOU WERE FILLED? Do you remember the first time you spoke in another language…when you spoke in tongues? I remember the first day I GOT IT! *I've been through trials.* AND I'M STILL HERE!!!!! *I've been through tribulations.* AND I'M STILL HERE! And it's because of the Holy Ghost! I will LIFT MINE EYES to the hills from WHICH MY HELP COMETH! My help cometh FROM THE LORD! I'M GONNA MAKE IT! I'M COMIN' OUT! YEA, THOUGH I WALK, THROUGH THE VALLEY OF THE SHADOW OF DEATH, I WILL FEAR NOOOO EVIL! BECAUSE THE HOLY GHOST, IS WITH ME! YES, LORD! YES, LORD! YES, LORD!

I was bent over in my seat and I couldn't stop crying. I thought about all of the times when I could have been dead. All of the times I could have gone crazy. All of the times I could have ended up like other women who were in 'that life' and how I could have gotten locked up.

I cried even more when I thought of how my mother would leave me in the car by myself while she used to go and get high. I thought about how it would take me three hours every morning to wake her up so I could eat breakfast. She would go into the kitchen and slam down the bowl, the spoon, the milk, and the cereal, then go back to sleep for another hour. She acted like she was mad at me for being hungry.

I thought about how I'd watched a twelve-year-old little girl cut a thirteen-year-old's jugular.

She died right there on the spot. I thought back to when a man robbed the store I worked at in the mall, and how he put a gun right to my side. I never feared a gun after that. I thought about John John raping me. I thought about how used I felt when I would sleep with men, with no strings attached. I really wanted to be loved. I really wanted to be with one man. I just didn't believe that a man would ever be faithful to me.

God had been there, waiting for me the whole time. He had patiently waited while I'd dogged him out and rejected him. All that time he still waited for me, patiently. I didn't even deserve God. He'd kept me all that time and I was mad at him. I was mad at him for making me go through everything I had gone through when other kids seemed to have normal lives. At that moment I understood that I went through a lot of those things because I didn't really want to be with God. It'd seemed too hard, almost impossible to be with him. But right then I needed him more than I needed food to eat.

"You neeeeed the Holy Ghost!" the pastor yelled. "If you don't have it, you're not going to make it. You may have recited the sinner's prayer...THAT AIN'T ENOUGH! O' LORD HELP ME PREACH UP IN HERE THIS MORNING! You may have recited...the sinner's prayer...and confessed with your mouth...BUT YOU GOTTA REPENT!!! And that means to be sorry and to turn away from sin. HAVE YOU RECEIVED THE HELPER SINCE YOU BELIEVED? WELL I'VE GOT IT! I'VE GOT IT!

AND I'M NOT GONNA LET NOBODY TURN ME AROUND!"

I had turned away from God. I began to cry again. I wasn't sure if I had the Holy Ghost. Everything was so crazy and I didn't know if I was going to make it out alright. I couldn't stop thinking about how I was going to make it.

"Now as I bring this thing on home," the pastor said, "Jesus said 'not only have I given you the Holy Ghost', but he says 'my peace I give unto you.' GOD has your peace! LET NOT YOUR HEART BE TROUBLED! YOU'RE GONNA MAKE IT! DON'T WORRY! DON'T WORRY! CELEBRATE! YOU'RE COMIN' OUT! GOD'S GONNA TURN IT AROUND! YES LORD! JOY, COMETH IN THE MORNING!

I didn't have peace. I knew God was calling me to be with him. I had known it even when I was little and was so excited about this "God" that people talked about. I didn't want their God, I wanted "THE GOD", the God who'd saved me the crazy night before, and the God who seemed to be calling out my name. I was tired of running.

"Will you come?" the pastor said. "I need somebody to pray. Maybe you need to come down for prayer, maybe you're not saved and you want to give your life to God. Will you come? Maybe you don't know if you ever received the Holy Spirit. Will you come?" The pastor kept repeating himself over and over.

With every tear I cried, it seemed as though I was slowly trying to let go of the past. I was letting go of everyone that hurt me, including people in the church. That day it didn't matter. I picked my head up and looked at the congregation with so many tears in my eyes that I could barely see. I had hope that there was more for me than what "this life" had to offer.

"Will you come..." the pastor continued.

I stood up out of my seat and began to cry again. Stacey started praising God when she noticed me get up. I could feel a shift, and I had enough energy to make it down the aisle. As I walked down the aisle, I could see the smiles on everyone's faces. Some people started to praise God like they knew me. They were happy for me.

I made it up to the altar and fell into the arms of an older woman who held me as I cried. I felt like I cried enough tears to form a river all around me. I was sorry for running away from God and for not even attempting to obey him all those years. I was especially sorry for not coming to him sooner...

God had never left. He had been waiting for me to come to him all along. When I came, he didn't remind me of how I had mistreated him, he accepted me just the way I was.

When God asked me if I would come, there was no other answer that I could think to **say** other than, **"YES,** Lord...**YES!"**

The entire church broke out into praise and a feeling of joy filled me. It was as if I had shown up in heaven for like fifteen minutes for a sneak preview of how it would be when I got there. I was so overwhelmed that I started dancing. I shouted and praised God so hard that I felt like I danced around the entire church. With every move, I felt as though I was shaking off every feeling that made me feel like I couldn't make it. The more I danced the more I knew that I was going to be okay. I wanted to feel like that all the time.

That morning I'd asked God to fill me with the Holy Spirit. And that's exactly what he did.

Chapter 24: Forever?

I stood there, watching Trina walk down the aisle in her white Vera Wang dress to "At Last" by Etta James. Trina was definitely known to spruce things up a bit. She definitely wouldn't do "Here Comes The Bride."

She seemed like she was floating down the aisle. Her strapless gown flared out like those dresses you wore when you were like five. It had a flower made out of material at the top right where her chest was, over her breast. It was the prettiest wedding dress that I'd ever seen. She looked like a princess. She wore this really pretty square cut diamond cross necklace we'd picked out from DeBeers, and she carried a bouquet of white roses.

All of the bridesmaids had on light purple Vera Wang cocktail dresses that stopped way past the knee. The dresses had really pretty bows that draped down the shoulders, and the front was a v-neck that really flattered everyone's shape. Everyone wore matching light gold strappy designer shoes.

I was the maid of honor, so I wore a really pretty cream dress that stopped right past my knee, and a cream flower in my hair. Stacey did my hair in a really pretty up do with curls that sort of formed a bun. I carried a bouquet with purple flowers. Unfortunately, Tre' was the best man.

It had been a couple of months since I had re-dedicated my life to Christ. I knew that the day was going to be a "trying" day for me. It was the day that I was going to stop running and look everything and everyone in the face, for good.

My mom and dad, Ernest and Janice, flew out to attend the wedding. It would be the first day that I had seen my folks since I'd left for L.A. We would talk sometimes on the phone, but I would purposely hang up the phone after around ten minutes or so. I actually looked forward to being around my folks again. I missed them. It's funny; no matter how 'off-the-hook' your family is you never stop loving them. You may not want to be around them all the time, but you still miss them. That is the craziest thing to me.

It was a small wedding with no more than one hundred people. They wanted to keep everything small and family oriented. Plus, I don't think Lord really wanted a lot of his family there. On the low, I don't think the Parkers wanted a lot of their family there either.

I watched Trina and Lord Life exchange their wedding vows. Pastor and First Lady Parker sat on the front row, dressed to impress. Mrs. Parker was crying all hard like it was a straight up funeral. The way she was acting, I was surprised that she hadn't worn all black. She looked more like she was in mourning than a glowing mother-in-law to be. The only thing that was glowing was Pastor Parker's face, which was so red that you would've thought he had gotten a tan that went bad. Pastor Parker looked like he had just eaten a big ol' bowl of earwax. It was obvious that the Parkers weren't too happy about Trina's wedding day.

"I do," I heard Trina say. Her eyes were all teary.

I started to tear up a little too. I was happy for Trina as long as she was happy. It seemed like she was going to have it all for the rest of her life: fame, money, and adoration. But at that point, I knew better than to totally believe that. Not being negative but that's just real. Does anything in this world last **forever?**

"I do," Lord Life said. He had a single tear running down his face.

As soon as everyone saw Lord cry, everyone was crying. I guessed everyone was in shock that he was crying, even if it was just a teardrop. He looked really vulnerable up there, looking at Trina while they expressed their love for each other. It was beautiful. In a world that's so greedy and hopeless, weddings can be the most beautiful things to watch. For one moment you see two people vulnerable and open to the possibility of something great.

I wondered if Trina was ready to stop playing her games. According to her, it was full force. I guessed I'd just have to see, because she was totally into Lord.

"You may kiss the bride," the preacher said.

"Aw...." everyone sighed, like a well-rehearsed choir.

Everyone stood up and clapped as Trina and Lord turned around to walk out of the door and into a life where they were now one. Trina was now the first lady of the man who everyone called a "Hip-Hop God", even though I knew that the Parkers hadn't expected that type of "first lady" to be in their daughter's future. I guessed they'd have to get over it.

In all the excitement, Trina gave me that wink of approval that I knew all too well. That was the last time I saw that look of approval. I literally watched the woman who had been my best friend since we ran the streets in B-more walk away to be on top of the world. While she was going into a world that was larger than life, I was leaving behind a life that had tried to kill me. We were going in opposite directions.

I had no choice but to join hands with Tre' as we walked down the aisle together. All through that entire wedding process I'd been praying to God that he would keep my tongue and my composure. That forgiveness thing was something else. I'd had to admit that we were *both* in the wrong when we slept with each other. But that still didn't change the fact that I really didn't want to hold his hand. Trina knew she could have just made me a bridesmaid instead of the maid of honor. I would have gotten over it.

After the ceremony and picture taking in front of the church, we drove over to the reception at a restaurant in Malibu that had a crystal clear view of the water. Only in L.A. was it perfectly normal to have a wedding reception by the water in December. Once we pulled up to the restaurant, we all scooted down a hallway of seats in a new custom-made, stretch Rolls Royce Phantom, (it wasn't even out on the market yet). The driver grabbed my hand as I stepped my feet out onto the pavement. After all of the bridesmaids were out, we walked inside.

We waited inside the waiting area for the wedding party to be called. I looked across to where the groomsmen were standing and Tre' was looking at me with that stupid innocent look on his face. He could really save all of that for his next victim.

"Lady B. Moore and Tre' Williams," the announcer called.

Tre' grabbed my hand and we started to walk in. It seemed like the longest walk I'd ever taken in my life. Most women probably thought that I was "doin it" by walking into a wedding reception with the hottest R&B singer on the charts, but I would have given up that spot easily—no questions asked. Of course I didn't have anything against Tre', but that didn't mean that I liked being around him. I was new at the whole "loving your enemies" thing. To me, Tre' was a *cold* piece.

"I missed holding your hand," Tre' whispered to me as we walked.

"I don't miss you holding my hand," I said, with a quickness.

"Trina told me you be actin' all holier than thou now. We'll see how long that lasts." Tre' looked at me to see my reaction. When he noticed that I wasn't bothered by his lil' funky comment, he dug a little deeper so that he could say something that would cut me on the inside.

"You can't hide behind this lil' religion thing you're on. One day you'll mature and you'll see that all this traditional stuff in the church doesn't matter. Maybe then you could be with me."

"Who says I even want to be with you?"

"Your lil' mama down there that be callin' my name in the middle of the night."

"Fu…" I had to catch myself from cursing his narrow behind out. I took a breather and took a moment to get some clarity.

"Friends, right?" I said instead, smiling at how that comeback was the work of a genius. I said it so nicely that I surprised myself. "You must have gotten me mixed up with another one of your *friends,* because that definitely wasn't me calling your name. Is your name Jesus? Oh, I thought not."

I showed no emotion and left him with a dumb look on his face. He had just officially gotten cut. We dropped hands and sat at the table reserved for us. It was time for me to go on the bridesmaid's side and it was time for him to go sit down, somewhere, out of my face.

I kept praying the whole time. The old me would have cussed him straight out by then. I was like two seconds off of laying Tre' out. It was kinda cool how I was able to get my point across and I really didn't have to say a word. He looked like he was burning up inside because I hadn't given into his little emotional roller coaster. That was one of my first lessons of saying something without really saying anything at all. It was tight.

As the night went on, I drifted into my own little world. I thought about God and how good he was. My new life wasn't easy, but I had hope that things would get better as time went along.

I sat back and just observed everything and everyone. It seemed like the things going on all around me during the wedding reception were part of a silent movie playing as I watched. It was almost unreal. It was unreal because, even though I was in the midst of everything, I didn't feel like I was a part of it at all.

Finally, as the night went on, I was able to go into the crowd and meet the people who needed to get acquainted with the new me: my parents. I say "new" because I was open to us being a family again. The old me wouldn't have even given them a moment of my time.

"Hi, daddy," I said. I looked at my dad, as his eyes got a little glassy while he looked at me. It was a look that told me that he missed me. A look that said "I'm sorry." A look that said he was happy to have the little girl that adored him so much back in his life. We hugged.

"Hi, mommy," I said, turning to my mom. Mom smiled, and in her smile I saw relief because she knew that I wasn't running away anymore. I'd been praying that my mommy would stop running and hiding behind the alcohol. However, that night there would be an open bar with some really high-end liquor.

"Hey, babbbbyyy," she said. Moms was lit. I looked past the smell of alcohol on her breath and the fact that she breathed really hard in my face when I hugged her. I saw a woman who had done the best that she knew how to do. She was hanging in there. Becoming a woman myself, I understood her pain. Some people bear it and get past it but a lot of people don't. I prayed that one day she would be able to get past it, just as I was learning to do. She had hung in there so that I could have a fighting chance. Even though things didn't seem like they were changing much, I was still going to continue to pray.

Moms was a tad bit drunk that night. But hey, there would probably be more than a hand full of folks who were going to be drunk right along with her. As usual, no one would notice that my mom was a functional alcoholic. That night my mom was "MY MOMMY." There was nothing that she could do to make me not see her as anything else but that.

My parents and I didn't really talk that much. We just enjoyed being around each other. We didn't need a lot of words. Even though we didn't really have a lot to say, we all knew that things were slowly getting better. Most importantly, I was slowly learning another definition of true love: patience.

They say that everything happens for a reason. I was starting to see that God had separated us for a while so that all of us could have time to heal. Especially me.

Chapter 25: Forever.

I drove down the 405 Freeway, blastin' "Imagine Me" by Kirk Franklin. It had been a long time since Trina's wedding and a lot had changed...including me.

As the wind blew my hair through the windows, I couldn't help but think about how I felt when I had gotten baptized six months earlier. I could still remember how I felt when I let everything in the past go down in the water, and how I came back up and out of the water into new beginnings. I had first gotten baptized when I was ten years old. I really wanted to get baptized again since I had more of an understanding of what a relationship with Christ really meant.

I cruised into the fast lane as my CD player changed to play "It Feels Good" by The Ambassador off of Cross Movement Records in Philadelphia. I had gotten into Cross Movement when my friend Melva from Brushfire Studies let me hold one of her CDs. She and my friend Spencer were constantly talking about how good their music was. I also found out that Spencer was from B-more too. We both had this unsaid understanding about our new lives as Christians, because coming from B-more we understood the hell, (and I'm not cussing), we had to go through in order to get saved. I used to think that Gospel rap was corny until I started listening to The Ambassador, Da' Truth, Phanatic, Flame and others from the label.

To my surprise, I also found other hot artists that spread the gospel on MySpace, such as Rob Hodge, LeCrae, Trip-Lee, Grits, KJ-52, Canton Jones and others. I would sit at my computer for hours, being exposed to another life as I was discovering even more new artists. I also loved Tonex's CDs. I would play his second CD, "O2", over and over again. I also kept Tye Tribett's CD in my player as well. And I LOVED Fred Hammond and Deitrick Haddon!

I had started going to Brushfire Studies with Stacey on Friday Nights and was on my way there. It was a citywide gathering on the campus of Faithful Central, where young men and women got together and talked about living for Christ on Friday nights. Going there, I found out that there were even more weirdo's like Stacey and I who were talking about waiting until they were married to have sex and doing other things to live for God. I guessed I was a weirdo then too because I was waiting. I had been celibate for seven months. *Yeah*, it was hard, but I was totally relying on God to "keep" me in every area of my life.

A lot of things were revealed to me when I abstained from sex and spent one-on-one time with God. I realized that when I was with John

John, I had sort of made him my God. I had relied on him for everything: food, clothes, money, happiness...everything. Eventually he failed me just like my father, and he wasn't really the man I thought he was. I had expected too much from John John *and* from my father. I had expected them to be perfect. Only God was perfect. God never failed. God had been doing things for me those past couple of months that made me trust him even more. *I* hadn't been all that perfect in my relationships, either. How could I have been faithful to someone that I *could* see, when I couldn't even be faithful to a God that I *couldn't* see? My relationship with God was teaching me how to be a better woman. I was slowly learning that I was **more than just an ordinary woman**...

I was learning that I was worth more than what I thought I was when I used to act like I had it all together. I really had low self-esteem. If I really knew who I was, then I would have understood that everything about me was priceless—including my body. Sex was good but my body wasn't my own. It belonged to the Lord. If I could keep myself for God then I could keep myself when the Lord blessed me with a husband. And honestly, I wasn't really concerned with getting married at that moment. I would be lying if I said that I didn't have my moments and that it didn't get a little rough. But hey, God was keeping me. One day at a time.

I even stopped cussin' like I used to. I realized how powerful words are. It was more than being able to say, "I haven't cussed in six months." It was about me not wanting to speak things that weren't going to bring any good. I'd had so many people tell me things that had caused me grief that I didn't want to do that to anyone else. Being that God was in me, I found myself talking more like him. I didn't totally understand everything yet, but I was learning. It is a day-by-day process. I understood what Stacey meant when she had said this.

Yes, I'd even started going to church regularly. To be honest, I actually wanted to. I realized that I needed more of God to be everything that I was called to be. Things weren't always perfect and neither were the people. However, I still wanted to go. It really helped when I joined Tabernacle of Praise Worship Center. I really appreciated the fact that Pastor Rhone would preach the entire truth, even if it seemed like it was something that no one really wanted to hear. I didn't want to play with God.

Obviously, there were some other people who didn't want to play with God either, because we didn't all walk out when we heard the truth. He would tell us straight up, no sugar coating anything. Even though I was sort of new, everyone seemed to treat me like family. I wasn't really used to that type of church. I could get used to it, though.

I learned that just because a person went to church every Sunday didn't mean that they were going to go to heaven. It was about having a relationship with Jesus Christ and seeking to please him everyday. In order to please him you had to know him. I started reading the Bible more.

Plus, the closer I got to God, the more I realized that it wasn't about me. I attended church to be more of service and also to praise God with other believers. I looked forward to thanking God. There was something about everyone getting together in church to praise God.

Sometimes I laugh at it all because I never would have thought that *I* would be the one not cussing and the one waiting until marriage to have sex. I wasn't even sure how I was going to get married and who the man was going to be. To be honest, all I really cared about was peace, joy, protection, and a sane mind. When it came to men, I learned that it was okay to be *friends* first—it's actually better that way. Most of the time, you never really get to meet the real person when feelings and other things are involved. I was tired of meeting men's representatives. When you were friends, eventually the real person would come out. I actually had some "brothers in Christ." (I actually used that term—funny, huh?) We were brothers and sisters because we didn't want to do things that would cause each other to fall. Our main concern was pleasing God. I never thought that I would be carrying around a Bible and reading it for real. I would even tell other people about Christ when the opportunity presented itself.

I started teaching children's dance classes at the Debbie Allen Dance Academy here and there to make some extra money, and also started dancing on tour with some of the most talented and known gospel artists in the country: Kirk Franklin and Mary Mary. When I danced on their tour, I was able to dance better than I'd ever danced before. Some people knock dancing for Jesus, but I knew that I was praising God when I was up there. God knew it too. People didn't know where I came from. It's a miracle that I even wanted to dance for God like that.

That night, I pulled up to the Bible Study, parked my truck and walked in. I was a little late and they had already started. Everyone was sitting around in a circle as usual, and I was waving at people here and there. We were always happy to see each other after a whole week of being misunderstood by people who just didn't understand why we were so serious about serving God. I found a seat next to my girl Stacey. Stacey and I had really become friends. We had our moments when we wouldn't agree, but she was always there to pray with me. She never told me advice that would hurt me, even if it was something that I really didn't want to hear. *"You can do better than that Lady," I could hear her say. God has more in store for you --just wait on the Lord."* I would tell her things about my life and about things I had done, and expected that she would treat me differently. She would always say that I wasn't telling her anything that she hadn't already heard or done before. She didn't stop loving me, despite my flaws. She would always tell me to put my trust in God instead of man. She was such a blessing in my life. I started talking to some women here and there about this new life, just as Stacey had been talking to me. It felt good.

I'd even begun to say to people, "God is going to do something great and new in L.A....you just see." I knew it was true, because he was already doing something great in me. I'd been inspired to do some new things with dance that had never been done before. I hadn't been trying to do what everyone else was doing. I wanted to do something different, something that no one had ever seen (including myself).

I was excited to see how God was going to move in the Entertainment Industry and use it as a means to tell stories that had never been told before. Stories that would change lives, dancing that would change lives...like he was changing my life day by day. It had already begun with some of the Christian based movies that had been coming out from time to time. I even heard that there was a book out about a young woman who got saved, and it really exposed the things that no one else wanted to talk about. The character was even from my hometown, B-more! I couldn't wait to get my hands on that book.

I was happy that God was doing great things like that because I wanted everyone to experience the life that I was living everyday with Christ. People needed to know that Christians weren't always saved—everyone has a B.C. (before Christ) story. If God could do it for me, then I KNEW he could do it for someone else. More importantly, God was getting his people ready for the rapture. The world won't last forever, but I have hope that I will last forever as long as I stay close to Jesus.

I'd seen how hard people worked to get money, cars, fame, and fortune. They worked so hard and when it's all said and done, it's just temporary. Even though I didn't have a lot of money, I felt like the richest person in the entire world. I had this joy and peace that "things" just couldn't give me. While some people made fame and money their Gods, I only wanted to make God my "God".

I truly believe that he is calling people to rise up and work for him harder than people work for a paycheck and a record deal. God wants people who are going to sell out for him...more than they will for the things of this world. He wants people who have faith that if they serve him with all of their hearts, that he will give them the "things" that money can't even buy. Money is nothing to God. I wanted to be one of the few that answered his call.

If that meant I had to be in the gym faithfully, wake up at 5 a.m., pray without ceasing, read the Bible when I didn't feel like it, then that's what I was going to do. If that meant not giving into sexual temptation, loving my enemies, saying "no" to dancing in a way that I knew wouldn't please God, then that's what I was going to do. If I had to say "no" to some opportunities that I knew wouldn't glorify God...then that's what I was going to do.

God has done MORE for me than what the entertainment industry could ever have done. My purpose wasn't just to "dance"...my purpose was to help someone else get to know Jesus through dance. In everything I do, I honor Him. I had to say "no" to a lot of offers because I didn't want to be the hypocrite that once turned me off from having a relationship with this wonderful God. It hasn't always been easy, because sometimes I don't know how I am going to get the rent paid. However, God has never failed me, and he's always provided as long as I've stayed faithful to him. This world isn't going to last **forever** and neither are the things in it. I have hope in Jesus and faith that there is a life after death. Who wouldn't want to live **forever?** I know I do. Like I said...God is going to do some great things in the city of Los Angeles.

It hadn't even been a year, and I was amazed at what God could do and will do. Since I made up my mind to live for Christ, things had slowly gotten better. Even though it'd been hard, I'd also been able to be "okay" with not having any hot dates on Friday nights. I actually enjoyed going to Friday night Bible Study. (I know, sometimes it's hard for *me* to believe).

Trina and I didn't really hang out that much anymore, and I'd been praying for her when she came to mind. She didn't call me as much because she always said that I talked like I was walking around with a Bible in my hands. Well, if she knew everything that I'd been through, she would be talking like she had one in her hands too. I still loved her.

A lot of people who heard that I was a Christian had lil' things to say here and there — sometimes it hurt at first. I learned that as Christians, we experience the things that Jesus did when he was on earth. Well, they killed him and hung him on a cross, so I guessed I couldn't really complain about people just talking bad about me. Some people seemed to be upset about my "change." I guess that was expected too. People don't really believe that I, or anyone else, could change. I understand why not. I didn't really believe that people could change either until God changed me. Sometimes it's something you have to experience for yourself in order to believe it. God is real.

I'm learning the real love thing, and it's way different than what I thought love was before. I'm learning to give and not expect anything back. I'm finding that God gives more than what anyone else ever could. Speaking of which, I've been tithing lately. My dad would be happy to hear that information.

Going back to that night at Bible study, a familiar face appeared as we all sat around the circle. It was Louis: the nice looking guy from the gym. He walked into the room, interrupting my thoughts. It must have been his first time because I had never seen him there before. He took his seat and listened to people talking about what they had gone through during the week, and what God was doing in their lives.

I stared at him really hard. He must have felt me looking at him, so he looked up and saw me smiling. Louis smiled back with a look of surprise. We weren't flirting, (even though he was still *fine*), but I was just happy to see him. From the look on his face, he was obviously happy to see me, too. We both took our eyes off of each other and paid attention to what everyone else was saying during the discussion. I was curious to know if he was still interested in me like he had been that day at the gym, but I figured that I had been doing well during the past seven months. I decided to just chill and wait to see what the Lord had to say. Not saying that I was thinking about sleeping with him, but I just didn't want to do anything that wasn't in God's plan. I had learned that the hard way.

There are things that another person just can't give you. Only God can make you feel like you're not alone when you sit in your house without any company. For once, I'd begun to feel content. Don't get it twisted—things weren't perfect around me, but I was okay with it. God has made things perfect within me, even though I was surrounded by imperfection. I didn't quite know every step that I was going to take, and I wasn't even sure how my next day would be. But I was okay.

I knew one thing, my new relationship with Jesus was helping me to become even more than what I ever thought I could be. I finally felt like I was getting closer to living up to my name. The name that my mother carefully selected, and the name that God gave me, because he always knew

who I was...who I am...and who I will always
"Be"...

Lady B. Moore

LIFE BEGINS WITH

GOOOD BOOKS™

And the BEST book is the Holy Bible...

MORE:
Words from Tova

Hey you!

I don't believe in coincidences. I truly believe that everything happens for a reason. It's no mistake that *you* "happened" to pick up *this book*. You're chosen!

I always knew that I wanted to "Be More." Even now, there's more for me to become. I remember knowing that I was going to be more even when I felt worthless, unappreciated, hopeless, and a failure. There was always something near, calling me closer to become who I was really destined to be. That "thing" was a personal relationship with Jesus Christ. I didn't start becoming who I was called to be until the day I decided to start a friendship with Jesus.

I remember thinking that I couldn't do the "Christian" thing, and that I couldn't live the life that God talked about. I specifically remember thinking, "How can I, as filthy as I am, live a holy life?" I admitted that I couldn't do it.

Well, that was the greatest revelation that I ever had. The truth was, I couldn't do it. It wasn't until I was truly saved, and filled with the Holy Spirit that I was able to see the true power of God. Things have been on the up and up ever since I invited God into my life. God does it through us. All he wants is for us to be willing to come near him. The more I got closer to Jesus Christ, the more I began to really experience life. There is a "real-life" where hope and miracles truly exist.

God is everything to me. My company if I'm lonely, my provider, my protector, and the list goes on. I really didn't think he could take a little girl from Baltimore, MD and make her into something that he would use to do great things.

I've talked to people, and they think that they need to stop doing whatever they are doing first in order to come to God. What I've found is that God wants you just the way you are. Once you receive the Holy Spirit and develop a personal relationship with Jesus, you will become more like him. He will make you more, as long as you want more of him. You will wake up and find yourself a person who is changing every single day.

You can start by saying this prayer and mean it:
I am a mess. I want to be MORE than who I am. I need you Jesus. I truly believe that getting to know you through a personal relationship is the only way to be saved. I want to know

you. I truly believe that you died for me and took on the sins of the world so that I could be saved. Through your death and your perfect blood, I am able to live a changed and "set free" life. I am truly sorry for everything I've done in the past that displeased you. Lord, I invite you into my life to make me new. Please fill me with your Holy Spirit, so that I can overcome the things of this world. I truly want to experience the good things that you have for me. I want more of you. I know that if you are in me, then anything is possible.

I am truly excited for you and your future! I know that from this day forth you will never, ever be the same. You have just begun your journey of becoming **MORE**. I love you!

In His Love,

TOVA

I'm Getting HIGH
©2006 by Tova

Woke up this morning
Wasn't sleep but I woke up this morning
It's a new day
This time I'm not gonna miss the SON shine
I'm getting HIGH
And I'm gonna continue to get HIGH, until I get lifted
And anything in contact with me is getting HIGH
Cause I'm not goin' down
I'm getting HIGH
At first,
I wasn't trying to experience this
Feelin this state of Joy and Peace, even though everything around me was dead
I didn't want to leave things alone
I didn't want to be alone
It would be YOU and I
Getting HIGH
HIGHER than smoke
HIGHER than chronic
HIGHER
You opened my mind up to greater things
I'm more creative when I'm with YOU
I'm more relaxed, confident…
Getting HIGH.
I couldn't afford to pay the price to get YOU
So I decided to give you my life
I'm happy I did
Cause that's how good you ARE
Since then,

I've experienced those things that go beyond what
they understand
You're so good, I had to share you
I had to tell them how much of the bomb you are
You got that sticky icky that makes me wanna
stick with you
They ain't ready
Cause you cost a price that can't be paid
You actually paid for ME to get HIGH
See…
The only way I can get HIGH
Is if I look past my struggles, pain, hurt,
temptations, sin…
My Cross
And see YOU
YOU were getting HIGH
Way before I was born when you
Took on the sins of the world
Died and rose again
And since I've been getting HIGH off of you,
You're all up in me
My clothes, my hair, my talk, my walk
I can't walk away from you
Even when I cry
Even when it seems like I can't do it and it hurts
Even when they don't understand how much I
pay to be with you
I can't walk away from you
So the demons telling me I'm not good enough
HIGHER
Fear
HIGHER
Depression

HIGHER
To those telling me I've got to open my legs in
order for a real man to open his heart
HIGHER
Lust
HIGHER
Diseases
Addictions
Loneliness
Low Self-Esteem
The enemy
HIGHER
Satan can't duplicate what you have
No chronic in this world can compete
Your HIGH is everlasting
They hunger for temporary things
And they wake up when it's over
I woke up for life to begin
I'm glad I saw your light this morning
I hunger for you more than a crack head feens…
Pick me UP Jesus
I'm getting HIGH

Thank you!
The Speech...

Lord...I can't get this thing started without you! To My Almighty God, My Lord and Savior Jesus Christ and my best friend for LIFE! Your will...not mine...Thank you for the cross...thank you for the trials, thank you for the suffering...your worth it! Thank you for your protection, wisdom, and thank you for the love that no one else can give...

To the man of God who planted the seeds, watered them, and watched them grow...Thank you for being my "Dad" in Christ and my #1 Supporter next to God. The fight continues!!! I could never repay you...

To Pastor David A. Rhone and the Tabernacle of Praise Worship Center family...Words cannot express how thankful I am for you...I LOVE all of you! Pastor Rhone, your willingness to give unselfishly from week to week is a true blessing to the entire family. You stepped right in without hesitation to provide the sermon for this book, no questions asked. Thank God for your faithfulness, passion for Christ, leadership, and love. Pastor Eric...Higha! Higha! Mother Genevia Jones...and all the Mothers...thank you for being available and willing to serve. Evangelist Kim Bryant, your talks and encouragement were priceless...praise God for you sis! I appreciate the true support and love...thank you for putting up with me during this process. Sis. Shonta...(Okay!?)

Terrina Scott with Minor Details Productions and Erika Braxton-White with Sullivan White Public Relations...your willingness and excitement to work with me was priceless! Thank you for seeing the vision.

Beth Payne, thank you, thank you, thank you...the seeds you plant in the industry aren't in vain. Beautiful woman of God...yes, you are!

Brother Gary Randolph!!!!!!!!! Praise him!!!!! I love you so...thank you for seeing the vision! I get excited when I see yours! God is doing great things in your life...not only do I believe it, but I see it! Everyone else will too. Brother Tionne Williams...thank you, thank you, thank you for being there at the right place and at the right time...had me hoppin' around on one foot praisin' Him over the phone in my Living Room (they don't know!) You are so wonderful...I love you! Sister Nicole, I get so excited when I think about your talents and your love for God...I'm so happy we are friends. Hold fast to the promises and keep up the fight...it's never in vain. Mytika...Love you sis!!!!!!!!!! You are so supportive and "real" (I need like another week...LOL!)

Brushfire Bible Study thank you for being on fire for God. Sister Deborah...I love you Pooooo! The virtuous woman wins!!!!!!! Ron G...remember that prayer? Let em' use ya! You better GO...*you best clean comedian in the world you*! Chris, Phil, and Derek...love y'all! You all are awesome men of God who are doing great, great things! My brother Phil and you're beautiful fiancé...I love you so...I praise God for everything God is doing in your lives. You have been sooooo faithful. Spencer, my brother...thank you for giving me the laptop that I used to write this book...your unselfishness is out of this world! (Yes. I put you on blast!) Rochelle Chatman...I love you Sis! Marvin Horn and family...I don't have to say anything...Praise God for everything he has called you to be, and how he is using you to build up his kingdom. You are truly my Brother in Christ...LOVE YOU!!!!!

Desadra "Dee-Dee"...my best friend who stayed my best friend through the years, the trials, the good, and the bad...I love you. Even when I would call you and say, "Can you loan me some money?" after not talking to each other for months, you wouldn't even trip. Money can't even buy a real best friend like you.

Angel...my best friend who has done so much...I love you! Thank your for flying 3,000 miles to support me. I am so happy that you are happy! "Western Girls put your hands up high!"

Thai Jones...I am really, really excited for you. *SANG!!!!* You KNOW the struggle. I know that God has amazing things for you. I truly want to see you to continue to shine!!!!! Get em' GIRL!!!!!!!! Thank you for being my Sis in Christ. Don't make me cry!!!!

Lenny a.k.a. Kel Spencer...thank you for being there to help a sister so many times that I stopped counting. Thank you for being apart of the very beginning. God is good. LOVE YOU Brother!

Sister Rochelle Chatman...I love you! Durrell Bishop, we've been through some real stuff. I could cry just thinking about it. I'm glad, because I got to know who you really are: an amazing brother. Tarik a.k.a. T.H. Moore, author of The End Justifies the Means...thank you for taking the time to help a friend. You have truly been an angel during the process. You helped with no questions asked. Troy Cole...you are so talented, and you have such a beautiful heart. You design the BEST covers! Thank you MeRhonda Ross for your patience!

Arena Players Youtheater: Mrs. Orange, Mrs. Charlene, Rodney, Troy Burton, Mrs. Yvette Shipley, Mr. Perkins, and the whole crew. Ericka Diggins...love you! Eric...wow! Broadway! You were always so talented. I am so happy I can call you a REAL friend. You never doubted. Robert Lee Hardy (A Keisha...). Robert...I see greatness! Remember Clifton Powell's Acting classes?

Adewole for stepping in selflessly and being a life-saver...God smiles on you. If I told everyone how great of a friend you are, and how much you've done, they wouldn't believe it. You're an angel.

Jaquay, and Jaquay's mommy…thank you so much! You are so loved. Consuela (Suki), Eric Pierce, and Shawn Samuels. Ryan Mitchner…Fire Squad…lol! To everyone in the class of 2001 at Morgan State University, and all who are blessed enough to have been able to attend one of (if not the BEST) HBCU's in the country! All the Morgan fam…you know you are loved. Floyd T, and the entire Mckeldin staff.

To Kevin and Frank Crosby who told me I should write when I first moved to LA. You guys have been one of my biggest supporters. Love you both! Thank you for always believing…even when it seemed dark and hopeless. You both know what I'm talking about…you've been there to see it all…I love you Perry and Doreen Pittman.

To Tara Thomas and Frank Ski who gave me my first intern at 92Q. Frank and family…I owe you guys some lobster…lol!

Black Enterprise Magazine: Earl Graves, Michael Graves, and Butch Graves. To Gale Hollingsworth who gave me a chance, because you saw something in me…Nichol Whiteman who gave me so many opportunities to shine…Natalie Hibbert who has been so supportive! Not too many people can say that they have worked for an organization that is a pioneer in our community, empowering our people by building wealth. Your trail has been a road map to so many!

David and Natalie at Our Weekly. Theresa Humphrey and family for your love and support…thank you! Kathy Williamson, thank you sooo much!

Los Angeles Sentinel: The Bakewells and all of my former colleagues. Krishna Tabor...I will not forget the "4 P's".

To Bill Duke and Sheila Moses. Sheila, thank you for taking the time to help those who reach out. Your kindness will never be overlooked. Mr. Duke, thank you for taking the time to meet with me at Howard University years ago to discuss my career...you are a rare jewel. Tim Hunter and Lynora Miller...Thank you! Love you both! Dick Gregory...you probably don't remember helping me, but I want everyone to know that you helped another without even a thought...thank you.

Thank you Marcus and Jaime King. You were soooo patient (smile) Jaime...I never forgot your words of advice, and I am putting them to use. Niles Kirchner...you're such a wonderful person...love ya! Phil Barner...you are the realest, most sincere person that I know.

Big brother Elvee, Will Nesbitt, Shyree, Bert, World on Wheels and the entire Get Lifted crew! Love you all!

My big sis...Sam "Baby Sam" Selolwane who never stopped believing...did I ever tell you that I love you Sammie? You are the hardest working woman in the music industry...you haven't been playin' since your days back when we were interns for Frank Ski. Dj Lil Mic..."Do the apple-scrap...Do the apple-scrap..." Not too many people can say that they are still friends after the good, the bad, the ugly, and the in-between. I praise God for you! Love you much!

Chelbi Harris…I can't even say what I want to say on here…words aren't enough. Just KNOW that I love you! Love you Sis! Quierra…Love you! **Sunny Fuller who never wanted to see me settle for anything less than more**. You are a true friend and the BEST Editor! Darryl Wharton and Dale for Thanksgivings I can still remember in LA. Pierre Johnson for looking out! Prince Rijan (you and this Hollywood name…lol)…love you babyyyy…for always being so supportive, honest, real, and loving. Aleysha Webster, CEO of Single Mom Magazine, thank you for the support!

Shauney Baby for being real, and I am so happy for you! Doreen Spicer-Danelly for your encouragement and always being available to help others. I love you so much! I'm blessed to call you a friend. Prof Keith Mehlinger for being one of the best teachers.

Kadija and Maurice for still being my friends through everything…you guys are amazing! I'm so happy that God joined two of the most sincere and loving people that I've ever met. Love you both! Aunt Glenda (Dee-Dee's Mom) for never forgetting my birthday, for taking the best pics, and for the best New Year's Eves I can remember!

To my fam' in LA: Marcus & Nikki Turner and family…you guys are true blessings from God. You took care of me, when everyone else walked away from me. You get to know who your friends are, when you're at your lowest "low". Regina, Walter, Breawnna, McKenna, Bakari, Momma Eunice, and Eunetta. God has blessed me with the BEST extended family I could ever have!!! WHAT!? Netta and Gina bean...I'm ready for some crabs!!!! Bakari...you KNOW I love you, even though you get on my LAST nerve!!! LOL!!!!! Mama Eunice...thank you sooo much for being a Grandma and a Mama to all those who need one. I love our talks Mama. I love you all so much...

*Hmmmmm...I think I am forgetting some folks...Hmmmm...***Mommy...did I remember to mention you?** LOL!!!! Just kidding!

To my Mommy, Laverne Cooper who has been "harassing" me to write a novel since she read my first book in Middle School...you are such a quiet strong woman and the best Mom I could have ever had on this earth...thank you for giving so unselfishly. You are so awesome Mommy and a wonderful Grandma! (I remember when you would find a way to make $5 work, and cook up a mean meal) You never gave up...you never stopped believing. You are truly a Lady...

To my Daddy, Frank Cooper who always told me I was "more" than what I thought I ever could be...thanks for taking me on my first dates. I know it was hard for you, but you have been much needed and you are much appreciated. I am so happy that you are apart of my life. I don't take that for granted. Gimme a kiss!

My Lil Sis' Stace' who is my #1 Supporter next to God, and one of the best Fashion Editors a writer can have. You are such an awesome woman. Keep overcoming. I see great things for you. Put God first, and see what will happen!

And another thing...I am so very proud of you. You're such a pretty, intelligent, and strong young woman. Get em'!!!!

My Lil' princess Nasya who is a light in my life...I love you forever, and Mommy wants you to be everything you are called to be. I love you so much. You are a strong and intelligent little girl. You are destined to "be more"! Remember...God loves you more than I could ever love you! Keep him first! Jesus is the way...don't ever, EVER forget that.

To my Grand Daddy (Nay) who was the reason why I completed college...your advice literally saved my life...heaven *has* to be smiling on you. Thank you for all of those quarters for frozen cups and trips to McDonald's to get sundaes... "Good Suga". One more thing...you were a "real" man...many are called...few are chosen...

Grannie (Mama Dukes) thank you for being a soldier...I am going to get your recipe for rolls down one day! Thank you for being there for me whenever I called. Not too many women can do what you do....Go Grannie!

Grand Daddy Cooper, thank you for taking me to church and for being there. Love you!

Grandma (Rhea-Rhea). You are so special! I didn't realize how special you were until I got older and realized that there aren't too many people out here like you. You are so giving and so kind. You are a ruby.

My Aunt Glenda who saved my letters from camp...(singing) *"Darling, nothing could ever change this love for you"*. My Aunt Cindy for giving effortlessly, Aunt Mary for taking me around town and showing important life lessons, Aunt Andy, Aunt Debbie for telling me about Jesus no matter what, and all of my family members who have had a part in this story we call life. Chapeio, I know you are going to do great things with any and everything you touch! I'm proud of you Chris for stepping out and starting your own business at such a young age. Most of all, *all* of my lil' cousins...I don't say it much, but I am proud of you. You inspire me!

Kirk Franklin...we've never met. But the sermon you preached at Faithful Central about looking past the cross and seeing the Father changed my life forever. Praise God for you and your beautiful family! Thank you.

To all those who I haven't mentioned that support and love me...

**To those who want to "B"-more...
This was for you...it's real...I'm a living
witness...**

Credits:

The term "Keep yourself" in **Chapter 18: Friends** is an actual term used by comedian Beth Payne in her stand up act. It is used by permission.

In **Chapter 23: Yes!**, Tabernacle of Praise Worship Center is an actual church under the pastoral direction of Elder David A. Rhone in Los Angeles, CA. For more info, visit www.topwc.org .

The sermon used in **Chapter 23: Yes!** is an actual sermon entitled "I Already Know I'm Coming Out", prepared and presented by Elder David A. Rhone. It is used by permission.

The phrase *"What you don't see is more real than what you do see."* is an actual phrase used by **Elder David A. Rhone.** It is used by permission.

In **Chapter 25: Forever** The song mentioned "It Feels Good" is an actual song by The Ambassador on Cross Movement Records. For more information on Cross Movement Records: www.crossmovementrecords.com .

In Chapter 25: Forever, Brushfire Bible Studies is an actual group that meets every Friday night in Inglewood, CA.   For   more   info,   visit www.brushfirestudies.org .

About the Author:
TOVA

In the beginning was the WORD... Introducing a writer who was called to write words that were predestined to be written since the very beginning. Tova emerges into the literary scene with her first novel, and she is ready to tell it all!

Tova was born in Baltimore, MD, as the first grandchild on both sides of the family. While her mom was pregnant, she was watching a movie and took notice of the name "Tova" in the movie credits. Because of its uniqueness, her mom chose that name. Tova, meaning "good" in Hebrew, grew up in Baltimore learning survival skills that most haven't experienced unless they grew up in an inner city where death is always right around the corner.

Tova always had a way with words. Being creative was something that she could use to express herself and escape the reality of being surrounded by drug addiction, alcoholism, and other things that she noticed were destroying the adults around her. Even then she knew she had a

HIGHER calling. Realizing that it takes more than imagination to escape the trappings of this world, she came face-to-face with the Truth.

Now, after many experiences, she has many stories to tell and a testimony that can cause an unbeliever to believe.

Tova is the CEO/Founder of Goood Books, a publishing company that is producing a new genre of books called "real life-lit" that tell stories about "real-life"...the hard life that most don't talk about with a WAY of escape to a better one...a real one.

Tova is a graduate of Morgan State University and a member of the family of Tabernacle of Praise Worship Center. She resides in Inglewood, CA. She has one beautiful daughter.

She is currently working on her next novel: **"More Than a Woman"**, tentatively slated to be released in the Winter of 2007.

"Life begins with Goood Books."

We want to hear from you!
If you would like to contact the author Tova, to share how this book affected your life, or would like to receive more information on Goood Books, please contact:

Goood Books
P.O. Box 91712
Los Angeles, CA 90009
gooodbooks@gmail.com
www.myspace.com/tovaonline

For more information on Tabernacle of Praise Worship Center or if you would like to attend worship service, please visit:

www.topwc.org

For more information on Brushfire Bible Study or how to start one in your area, please visit:

www.brushfirestudies.org